In Search of Free Land

by
Arley E. Cooper

PublishAmerica
Baltimore

© 2007 by Arley E. Cooper.
All rights reserved. No part of this book may be reproduced, stored in a retrieval system or transmitted in any form or by any means without the prior written permission of the publishers, except by a reviewer who may quote brief passages in a review to be printed in a newspaper, magazine or journal.

First printing

ISBN: 1-4241-8740-0
PUBLISHED BY PUBLISHAMERICA, LLLP
www.publishamerica.com
Baltimore

Printed in the United States of America

Dedication

I dedicate this book to my grandson, Trace A. Cooper. who at the age of 6, after hearing me tell a story about his ancestors, brought to me a pencil. He then asked if I would write for him a story about our family.

Contents

Chapter One Boyhood Days 7
Chapter Two Willie Goes to Town 9
Chapter Three Big Sean Goes to Church 21
Chapter Four The Secret Is Out 30
Chapter Five The Temptation of an Apple 36
Chapter Six Love at First Sight 41
Chapter Seven Willie's Punishment 54
Chapter Eight Planning for the Big Trip 58
Chapter Nine Mark and Sarah Set the Date 62
Chapter Ten The Last Night Before Their Trip 70
Chapter Eleven West to the Blue Ridge 74
Chapter Twelve West Beyond the Blue Ridge 89
Chapter Thirteen On the Wilderness Trail 98
Chapter Fourteen Back to Virginia 108
Chapter Fifteen Mark Prepares to Leave for Kentucky 118
Chapter Sixteen Mark Leaves to Build Sarah a Home 121
Chapter Seventeen Prosperous Days on the Frontier 137
Chapter Eighteen Willie Becomes a Free Man 140
Chapter Nineteen The Exploratory Trip to the Illinois Territory . 142
Chapter Twenty Willie Leaves for Illinois 161
Chapter Twenty-One Mark and Sarah's Leave for Illinois 162
Chapter Twenty-Two Young William Moves to Illinois 166
Chapter Twenty-Three Death to the Legend of the Long Black Whip 171
Chapter Twenty-Four West to the Oklahoma Territory 173
Chapter Twenty-Five The Whispering Sounds from the Past 177

Chapter One
Boyhood Days

They could have been brothers except for one small detail, one was white and one was black. One was named Mark Harrison Cooper son of William of English decent who was raised on a farm near Mecklenburg County, Virginia. One was William named after his owner, he was of African decent and called Willie for short. The contrast between the two was as different as day light and dark on the outside but on the inside was a bond that would not allow the color of their skin to filter the dark from the light. In the process of growing up in the beauty of the Virginia hills, Mark became a good reader and had very good hand write for a boy of such a young age. Willie of course was not given the opportunity to read and write as a slave he was expected to grow up and to work in the fields and help there mom and dad so they could become more productive as a family. It was in this environment that William and Mrs. Cooper raised their family of seven and became wealthy.

In that distance valley of the past Mark and Willie played and worked together as boys. Then as they grew older they began to take on special characteristic that made their personalities stand out. Mark with his deep black wavy hair and snappy black eyes that seem to look through you if you dare to oppose his views. He was now growing into a young man with a tall slender body that carried a set of husky arms and shoulders. He had a thin smile that made him pleasingly pleasant to be around but always gave the appearance of being in control. Willie on the other hand was quiet different. He had dark kinky hair, big blue eyes and a smile that could turn tears into laughter. He was shorter then Mark and with his over size body he appeared to be much more stockier. Willie grew to admire Mark for his fairness to the slaves and Mark grew to admire Willie for his ability to laugh and smile even under the hard conditions of slavery.

Chapter Two
Willie Goes to Town

One morning the sun was peaking over the foot hills down into Willie's bedroom. He pushed open the window of the little slave cabin.

"Willie," a voice called.

"Get up, we're going to town," shouted Mark!

" Mom, Dad! I get to go to town with Mark. That means I don't have to work in the fields today," said Willie.

"Hush," said his mom as she set his morning breakfast of biscuits and gravy in front of him.

His dad was just leaving the cabin to go on the wagon to the fields with the other slaves when he turned to Willie and said, "Don't get too uppity and remember your place on the sidewalk and step aside to let the white folks by."

"Okay, Pops," said Willie with that big old smile. "I'll be so polite they'll think I'm white."

His dad just shook his head and walked out the door to go to work.

Mark came by the cabin to tell Willie to go harness up two of the horses in the barn and hook them up to the wagon in the storage shed. Mark of course had to stay and have biscuits and gravy with Willie's mom. Mark stepped out of the little slave cabin and started up to the big house where the team of horse and wagon was waiting for him.

As Mark climbed up into the wagon Willie was holding the lines to the team so they wouldn't run until Mark came. "Can I drive the team today?" he asked.

"Yes, Willie," replied Mark, "you can drive the team today but hold on to the lines tight for they are very high-spirited and will run at the drop of a hat."

Willie looked at Mark with a big smile and said, "Maybe they're kinda like you, Master Mark, the high-spirited part, I mean." Then he loosened the lines a little and said, "Get up," to the high-spirited team of horse as they tried to force their heads down so they could run. But Willie with his strong hands and arms brought them under control. Then as the wagon started to disappear around the corner from the big house you could hear the laughter as Willie shouted, "Can I run 'em now, Mark?"

"Yes, Willie," replied Mark, "but just for a short way."

Then after a short run Willie's large arms pulled back on the lines to bring the horses to a walk Willie turned and looked back down toward the farm where the house, barns and slave cabins were nested in the valley below. Willie looked at Mark and said, "Mark, I know I'm just a slave, but today I feel free!"

"Enjoy the moment," said Mark as he took the lines and put the horses into a trout.

Willie leaned back into the spring seat as he said, "I feel like a landlord." Then he laughed and said, "Take me to town, boy!"

"Yes, sir, Master Willie!" Mark said as he looked at Willie with that thin smile and black snappy eyes.

When they pulled into town Mark turned to Willie and said, "Willie, I have some business to take care for Dad so you will have to load the wagon yourself at the mill. When the wagons loaded drive up to the grocery store and I'll meet you there."

After Mark had step down from the wagon he reached into his pocket and pulled out three slips of paper. "This one," he said to Willie, "is for the order at the mill and this one is for the order at the store." Now Willie he said in a more controlled voice, "This one is to be keep in your pocket in case some one wants to know who you belong to. So don't lose it. Okay!" Then Mark said to Willie, "Whose names is on the mill order?"

"Mr. Conklin."

"Whose name is on the store order?"

"Mr. Lucas."

"Now don't let anyone know you can read," said Mark as he turned and walk away.

Willie drove the team down to the mill and handed Mr. Conklin the order. After Willie loaded the wagon Mr. Conklin said to Willie, "You tell Mr. Cooper that I'll see him Sunday for Mark's birthday party."

"I sure will, Mr. Conklin, sir," replied Willie as he left driving the team up the street to the grocery store.

Willie felt so important for he was driving a loaded wagon through town all by himself. He'd tip his cap to the ladies and say, "Good morning, ma'am." Then he'd tip his cap to men and say, "Morning, sir." He would laugh with that big old smile, then he remembered what his dad said back at the cabin about not getting to uppity.

He was just pulling up to the store when a voice called out, "Boy!"

Willie turn to look and there stood the largest man he had ever seen. He looked to be well over six foot tall with long brown stringy hair under a coon skin cap. His frontier looking pants and shirt covered a large stout looking body that seemed to roar when he talked.

"Who do you belong to?" shouted the large man as he walked closer to the wagon.

"I's belong to Master Will Cooper, sir," replied Willie.

"Bring me a cup of water from that well," demanded the big man. "And hurry it up," he shouted. "I'm thirsty."

Remembering what his dad said, Willie went to the well and filled the cup hanging on the well with water from the bucket hanging from a pulley above the well and took it over to the big man saying, "Here you are, sir."

The big man took a drink of the water, spit it out, threw the cup at Willie and said, "Boy, you get me some cold water or I'll tan your hide good!"

That's when a voice in the crowd said, "Sean, it's best you let up a bit. You know Will Cooper won't take kindly to someone messing around with his slaves."

Then another voice said, "I think Mark's in town down at the bank."

Willie picked up the cup and walked back to the well washed it in the water that was in the bucket. Then he through the water from the bucket on the ground and drew a new bucket of water from the well. Handing the cup to the big man he said, "Here's your cold water, sir."

Then he turned to walk into the grocery store.

"Boy!" shouted Big Sean Davis the local town bully. "You come back here and give me those papers in your pocket now!"

Willie remembering what his Dad and Mark said walked back over to the big man and pulled the three pieces of paper from his pocket. He stuck the two for the orders back in his pocket and gave Big Sean the one that verified his Masters name. Big Sean looked at the one he handed him.

Then he looked at Willie and said, "Boy, how did you know which piece of paper to give me?"

Willie said, "I's just a dumb slave and I's can't read, sir. So I's bend the paper so I's knows which ones to give you."

"Willie couldn't keep from smiling because he did know how to read as Mark had taught him when they were little but only Willie and Mark knew. Mark had told Willie you can't tell any one not even your Mom and dad or you could be sold off to another owner and separated from your family if my dad was to find out."

Big Sean was furious by now as Willie was smiling, then he said, "Boy! You give me them other papers now!"

The words was still ringing in the air when Big Sean's head was pulled back and his body slung to the ground with such force that the air in his lungs was exhausted on impact to the ground causing a timid roaring sound.

When Big Sean Davis opened his eyes there was a black shinny boat forced across his throat to the extant that his eye balls began to bulge. There above him stood Mark Harrison Cooper a pitch fork gripped tightly in his hands. The metal tongs was pointing down with in a few inches of his eyes. Mark's black snappy eyes showed the extant of his anger as he spoke very clear and direct these words.

" Take a good look at the day light for if you make one move you shall see it no more!"

Mark turned then to the crowd that had gathered and said, "Let me make it clear to all concerned. The slaves from the Cooper farm will show ownership papers when asked and obey by the town laws. But we will not tolerate unnecessary abuse to are slaves. Do I make my self clear?" Mark said as he turned back to look down at Big Sean Davis.

Big Sean was by now gasping for air and trying very carefully to nod his head yes with out moving. Then as Mark took his boot away from Big Sean's throat two of Sean's friends helped him up.

A voice from the crowd said, "I know one thing I'm not missing with any of those Cooper slaves."

Then another voice said, "You know he's right, if we took are best horse to town I guess we wouldn't want some one a messing with it either."

The crowd was starting to move away when a third voice said, "You know that Willie hasn't been to town much, but when he does come to town he's all ways saying yes sir. And take a look at those arms on him, I bet he is a good worker too."

Big Sean was walking away with the crowd when he look back over his shoulder in complete disarray about what had just happened to him that day. He then saw Mark staring at him through cold black eyes that seemed to say *I dare you to challenge my authority.*

Mark looked over at Willie and said, "Willie, you go in and have that order filled then wait for me on the wagon until I get back."

"Okay, Master Mark, sir," said Willie as he grinned a little and walked into the store.

Mark started walking up the street when serval of the people in the crowd gathered around and was patting him on the back saying, "You sure showed that big bully, Sean Davis, a thing or two."

As they walked away one young boy looked up at Mark in admiration and asked, "Where you going, Mark?"

"I'm going to get Willie a birthday gift, he just had a birthday a few weeks a go and we were too busy in the fields to get anything for him," said Mark.

The boy asked, "Well, how old is Willie?"

"Eighteen," Mark replied.

"Then how old are you, Mark?" the boy asked.

"I'll be 21 tomorrow," replied Mark.

"Then how old were you when you became a man?" the boy asked.

Mark looked down at the boy with a larger smile then normal and said, "When I was man enough to stand up and be accountable for what I believe in."

The boy seemed contented with the answer as he hung his head and walked away.

Mark was just turning the corner and walking out of sight when Willie gave the store owner Mr. Lucas the order. Mr. Lucas had the order all filled except one item on the list that said Scott when you get done with the order let Willie pick out some candy for him self before he leaves. He had a birthday a few weeks back and has grown into one of my better workers. I'll see you Sunday for Mark's birthday party signed, Will Cooper."

Willie was just walking out of the store chewing on some candy when Mark came down the street with a package under his arm. Willie went over to the well and bought a nice cold cup of water back over to the wagon where Mark was climbing up on by then. Handing Mark the cup of cold water he said with a smile, "Here's your cup of cold water Master Mark. Sir!"

Mark looked at Willie and said with a thin smile on his stern looking face, "Come on, Willie, let's go home!"

Their wagon was moving slowly because of the heavy load when Willie looked over at Mark and thought to him self how lucky he was to have Mark as a friend and to be a slave in the Cooper family. He had heard some of the horror stories about the beating of the slaves by other slave owners. After he seen what had happened back in town Willie knew their child hood days were over and some day Mark would become his owner. He leaned back in the spring seat on the wagon with a contended smile and said, "Take me home, Master Mark, sir!"

They were about half way on the eight mile trip home when Mark pulled the team and wagon over to the side of the road.

As he stepped down, he said, "Willie, take the bucket down to the stream and get a bucket of water for the horses."

Willie took the bucket down to the stream and filled it. Then as he was holding the bucket so the horses could drink, Willie noticed Mark reading a news paper. "Can I read the paper when you are done with it, Mark?" asked Willie

Mark looked at Willie and said in a hesitant way, "Why do you have such a desire to read, Willie?"

"Because I can travel beyond my slave cabin and the farm so I guess it makes me feel free," replied Willie.

Mark's concerned look turned to a conservative smile as he said, "Then by all means, Willie, read the paper and enjoy the trip, but make it a short one as we have to be heading for home soon." Mark was thinking of what his dad had told him about how important it was that the slaves not to be allowed to read.

While watching to make sure no one saw Willie reading, he heard Willie say, "Mark! Mark! Did you see where there's free land out west of the blue ridge? Wouldn't that be some thing to cut a path into the unchartered wilderness like that Daniel Boone guy did?"

Willie's eyes was dancing with joy and Mark new his dad's greatest fear had come to past. Now that Willie could read so good he would for ever be trying to better him self in the endless search for freedom. *My God*, Mark thought to himself, *what have I done? What if dad finds out and was I right or was I wrong?* "Willie! The trip is over. Hand me the paper and drive the team home," commanded Mark in a stern voice.

The rest of the way home Mark and Willie didn't talk except for an occasional glimpse toward each other. Mark was trying not to come to a decision that he knew he'd have to make some day about what to do with Willie if and when it became public knowledge that he could read. Willie was trying not to make the decision about his endless desire to run away from the farm and follow his dreams.

The sun was at high noon when the sight of the farm and slave cabins came into view. The horses were sweating causing a milky white lather to form on their bodies where the straps of the harness rub against their skin from the heavy load and the heat of the noonday sun. They were at the last turn going down to the farm when the sound of the ever fath full dinner bell began to ring from the valley down below. The wagon had just came to a stop in fount of the water tank for the horses.

Mark looked over at Willie and said, "Let the horses drink a little but not too much then unhook them from the wagon, take them to the barn and give them their feed. I'll meet you here after dinner. Oh, by the way Willie, yes, it would be something to charter a path through that wilderness for other people to follow a specially if the land was free."

Willie's concerned look turn into a smile that reached all most from one ear to the other as he jumped to the ground and back up in the air again and said, "I'm so happy I could hug a bear."

Mark with a slight chuckle said, "Who knows, Willie, maybe that bear will be so happy to see you he may just give you a hug instead. You know that Daniel Boone guy said, 'When them there bears hug so tight that your eyes balls start to bulge it's called a bear hug,' but they only do that when they are hungry."

Mark turned to walk up to the big house for dinner as Willie's eyes got larger when he started to think about what Mark had just said. His big smile returned to his face as he walked from the barn up to his cabin for dinner. In the back of his mind Willie was thinking, *Ah, that Mark is just trying to scare me.*

"Or is he?"

There was a wash pan filled with water and a bar of lie soap laying there beside it in font of the cabin so Willie his dad and four younger brothers could wash their hands before dinner. Willie's one older sister would be eating at the big house as she worked directly for Mrs. Cooper.

Willie pushed the screen door open after he had washed his hands and said, "Mom! Dad! Guess what? Mark was reading a newspaper in town and he said there was free land out west beyond the Blue Ridge."

"Don't be talking about that free land stuff! Master Will treats us good and we don't want him thinking we want to be free," said his Dad as Willie sat down to eat his bowl of bean soup with a big helping of corn bread that his Mom had just made.

"Willie did you get to look in any of the store windows in town?" asked his Mom.

"No Mom," replied Willie, "I had to load the wagon by myself, but I did get to drive the team and wagon down main street. I tip my hat at the ladies and said morning Mam then I'd tip my hat at the men and said morning, sir. It was a good feeling too Mom. Then some thing awful happened. A big man said boy come here! He made me get water for him then he threw it at me and said he'd tan my hide if I didn't get him some cold water and show him my ownership papers. So I got him the cold water and I showed him the owner ship papers. Then he wanted the papers for the orders that Mark had given to me and before I knew what had happened the big man was on the ground looking up at Mark. I believe Mark would have hurt him bad if he had not obeyed ever word he said."

"You see what I mean about the Cooper's," said his dad. "And we ought to be thankful that we are not owned by someone that don't take care of their slave."

"Then I guess it's best we all get up and go back to work," replied his mom.

Mean while up at the big house Mark was having dinner with his family that was being served by Willie's sister Ann. She was given the middle name of Martha Ann Cooper, Mark's mom. Annie as she was called, was seventeen very attractive and seem to made the maid dress that she wore come alive when her fine structured legs moved her well developed body around the table to serve the food. She was of a more serious nature than Willie and only spoke when spoken to.

At the head of the table sat the stern sophisticated looking William Cooper, known to all as Will. When he talked everyone would listen. So as he bowed his head and said, "Dear Lord," the room became so quiet you could hear a pin drop. He then ended the blessing with theses words.

"We asked that you bless the food for are slaves, so that it may give strength to their bodies, love to their hearts and peace to their minds. We asked this in your name, for our sake. Amen."

"Mark, how did it go at the bank today?" his father Will asked as he raised his head, displaying a slight grin.

"Okay."

"Did you ask Mr. Getz for an application for a loan and did you fill it out the papers the way I told you to?"

"Yes."

"Well, did they okay the loan?"

"Yes, but not until you come in and sign the papers. Dad, why did you send me to fill out the papers when you knew that you had to sign before they would release the money?"

"That's a good question son now let me ask you a question. Did you fill left out of the important part of the family operations?"

"Well, I guess so."

"Now that you know how to ask for money, maybe you need to know more about how we intend to pay the bank back and can we realistically meet our obligation if I give you the power to sign for the loan."

"I guess I need to get more involved in the business end don't I Dad?"

"Yes, starting in the morning. Oh by the way did Willie get some candy at the store."

"Yes, enough to last a week if he don't eat in his sleep," replied Mark with a slight smile.

Every one at the table was laughing as Annie came back into the room to serve some more food. All of the Cooper family was at the table that day but only Mark was old enough to share in the decision making of the farming process. Mrs Cooper sitting at the other end of the table always new in detail the operation of the farm but only exercised her authority in the house hold decision making part. That included keeping in stock the food for the slave families so there energy level would be high enough to perform a honest days work.

"Dad," Mrs. Cooper said, that's what she called her husband Will when the kids were around, "we need some more corn meal for the slaves."

Mark spoke up and said, "Mom, I'll have Willie take care of that when he gets the wagon unloaded."

Will smiled a little and said, "Annie, we're ready for dessert."

After dessert Mary, Betty, Shirley, Samuel, Tom, and Matt. Mark's younger brothers and sisters asked to be excused from the table. As they were leaving the room, Mark said, "I guess I'd better get Willie to work before they talk him out of his candy."

Mark was getting up to leave the table when his dad asked, "Did Willie do okay in town today?"

Mark grinned a little and said, "Well, Dad, it was quite a sight to see Willie driving that loaded wagon down the street, tipping his hat to the ladies, saying morning, ma'am, then to the men and saying morning, sir."

Both his mom and dad were smiling as Mark left the room.

The dinner hour was coming to an end as Willie and Mark was walking in the direction of the water tank. There Mark would give Willie the orders for the afternoons work to be done. The rest of the slaves were leaving the six slave cabins to go to their work area for the afternoon.

As they walk by Mark and Willie they tipped their caps and said, "Good afternoon, Master Mark, sir."

Gossip in the slave camps in the early 1800 hundreds was an important part of their lives and of course by now most all the slaves new of Mark and Willie's trip to town and how Mark stood up and protected Willie. Their admiration for Mark and their envy of Willie grew after that day, for it was plain to see as the two boys took their first big steps into manhood that their childhood bond would not be easily broken.

The sun had just began it's daily trip below the Harrison beyond the blue ridge when the ever faithful sound of the dinner bell began to ring for the second time that day calling the weary slaves to come home. Then as they approached their tinny slave cabins chanting the legendry slave songs of the day, it seemed to bring a peace upon the valley that even the owners came to admire. The last light from the Cooper farm was turn out by Will Cooper as a day in the life of the Cooper family and their slaves came to an end in the year of 1808.

Chapter Three
Big Sean Goes to Church

It was Sunday morning, the sun was just coming up when out of the hen house strutted a cocky old rooster that sent out his overbearing but always faithful chronic crowing sound that made sure that all was up for the day. He would scratch the ground with first one foot and then the other as dirt would fly out behind him. He then strutted back and forth to impress the hens that was watching and stop long enough to do his famous *cock a doodle doo.* Shortly smoke began rising from the chimney indicating that the Coopers and their slaves were up for the day. The smell of bacon being fried in the old iron skillets filtered through the big house as a voice of Will Cooper was heard by Mark who was still in bed. The voice was saying, "Mark! Mark Harrison Cooper come a jumping its time to eat." Mark had been awoke from a deep sleep and the dream he was dreaming was beginning to fade. As he sung his feet over the side of the bed and sat there for a moment with his eyes closed he could still hear the endless distance sound of bells ringing. There were people gathered around staring at him, that gradually disappeared, when the sound faded completely.

 Mark got up dressed and came down the stairs. He walked into the dining room that was only used for Sunday dinner, special events and guess that would come to visit. There around the big table under a large chandelier sat the Cooper family and one guess as they sang in harmony lead by their guess Happy Birthday to Mark. Silence fell upon the room as the voice of Will Cooper said, "Time for the blessing."

The voice of their guest asked for the blessing the way he was taught by Will Cooper when he was a little boy and given the name of Willie. When Mark and Willie were little boys they played to gather a lot as Will only had one slave family at the time. So he allowed the little slave boy to have birthday breakfast with Mark and also allowed Mark to have birthday breakfast with the little slave boy. Will became fond of the little slave boy so he gave him the name Willie.

Their breakfast was coming to an end as Annie entered the room to finish serving coffee and drinks. When she was done serving she stop by Mrs. Cooper's chair and said, "Mrs. Cooper, ma'am, will you be needing anything else served for breakfast."

"No, Annie, you go and take the rest of the morning off, but be back to serve dinner at one o'clock, sharp," replied Mrs. Cooper.

"Okay, ma'am, and thank you," Annie said as she bowed her head slightly to show respect for Mrs. Cooper's authority.

"Oh, Annie, plan on being her all afternoon as we are having guest in for Mark's party," said Mrs. Cooper.

"I sure will, Mrs. Cooper," Annie replied. As she walked by Mark's chair, she said in a low voice, "Happy Birthday, Mark."

"Thank you, Annie," replied Mark. Then he said, "Annie, I told your mom I would take her to town someday so she could look in the store windows, so why don't you come with her if you can work out the time with Mom."

"Okay," said Mrs. Cooper, "we'll talk about it later."

Will remained silent, but with a concerned look on his face.

"Thank you, Mark," said Annie as she smiled at him and left the room.

Willie was now getting up from the table and said, "I reckon I best be going, too."

Mark, with a big smile on his face, said, "Willie, aren't you forgetting something?"

IN SEARCH OF FREE LAND

Willie's eyes began to get larger as he looked at Mark and said, "No, Master Mark, sir, I haven't forgotten, but after what happened in town yesterday I don't feel I should challenge you in any way, shape, or form. For I know now you've been letting me win at are annual arm wrestling contests."

"I'm sorry you feel that way, Willie, but maybe you're right, maybe it should remain a mystery as to who is the strongest," replied Mark.

Willie was starting for the door when Will Cooper laid his paper down that he was reading and said, "Willie," in a demanding voice, "come back here! Now tell me what happened in town yesterday that everyone except me seems to know about."

Willie was walking back in the direction of Will when he said as he looked over at Mark in concerned way, "Well, I don't know if I should say."

"Stop!" demanded Will. "Mark didn't ask you the question, I did and I expect an answer, now!"

"Yes, sir, Master Will, sir!"

"Do you know that Big Sean Davis?"

"Yes. Well, sir, I was going into the store and Mark was down at the bank when he yelled at me and made me bring him some water from the well. Then he threw it at me and said bring some cold water or he'd whip me. After I gave him a cold cup of water he made me show the ownership papers. Then he wanted to see the other papers for the orders that Mark gave me. That's when it seemed that Mark came from out of nowhere and threw that Big Sean Davis on the ground. He grab a pitchfork that was leaning against the wall where he fell and shoved his boot into his neck so hard it looked like his eye balls were about to pop out. Then with that pitchfork right over his eyes, Mark said, "You make one move and you'll see daylight no more and he didn't move a bit either, Master Will."

"Did Big Sean look at the orders?"

"No, sir, Master Will, he didn't get to."

"Okay, Willie, now before you leave you stop in the kitchen and see Mrs. Cooper. I think she has some good news for you."

Willie was heading for the kitchen as Mark scooted his chair back to get up when his father Will said, "Hold up a minute, Mark, we need to talk."

"Yes, sir," said Mark as he sat back down slowly in the chair.

"Mark, did Willie cover everything?" asked his father as he grinned a little.

"Yes, pretty much," replied Mark as he leaned back in the chair.

"Mark, I understand you being upset with this Sean Davis guy and I am proud of you for standing up for what you believe in. But I can't condone the way you handled the situation. I believe that violence should have been your last resort."

"Well sir, from what I've heard about Sean Davis is he likes to bull people around more then he likes to lessen."

"Son, do you know who this Sean Davis guy is?"

"No dad, but he does seems to be the town bully."

"Well I've heard about this Sean Davis his father said in a control toned voice. The word is that he has spent a lot of time the last few years in the frontier land out west of the blue ridge and has built a reputation of being a good hunter and man you don't want to cross. Some even say he has hunted with that Daniel Boone guy."

"Well regardless of who he is dad, he has no right in looking at our personal papers and when I was little I've seen you threaten to take the whip to a man in town once for less."

"Yes son but if you remember I didn't have to as we settled it with words."

"Yes, sir, but if I remember right you was doing the talking and he was doing the lessening," replied Mark with a slight grin.

"Mark, all I'm trying to tell you…"

Mark interrupted his father as he stood up, look him square in the eyes with out blinking and said, "Dad, I know you are concerned about me and what Big Sean might try to do to me. Well, if that does happen maybe I'll try your way then his black eyes snapped as he said and if that don't work I'll do it my way."

His father looked at Mark and probably for the first time realized his oldest child was not a boy anymore. He put his arm around Mark's shoulder and said, "Come on, son, there's one thing there's no dealt about. We both need to get dressed for church."

"Maybe that's way you didn't have to use that whip dad, you have a gift for choosing the right word at the right time," said Mark.

Then as they left the room his father said, "Son, the right word at the right time can change the world but a pitchfork in angry man's hands can blind one's views forever."

"I surrender, Dad, you win again," said Mark as they both left the room to go get dressed for church.

Mark and his father had just walked out of the dining room when they heard Willie in the small office room of from the kitchen area saying, "Thank you, Mrs. Cooper, ma'am, and you won't be sorry, either."

Mrs. Cooper had just told Willie about the surprise that she and Will had planned for him when Mark and his father Will stepped into the office room.

"Willie," said Will, "what's going on in here?" As if he didn't know.

"Master Will, sir, I's get to be an usher for the guest today and Mrs. Cooper says I gets to wear a special suit made just for me," replied Willie with a big smile that covered a large part of his rounded face.

"Mom," Will said to Mrs. Cooper. That's what he called her any time a family member was present. "Has Willie tried the suit on yet?"

"No, I was getting ready to have him do that when you walked in," replied Mrs. Cooper.

"I'll get it," said Mark as he walked over to the cabinet and pulled out a package.

"That's the package you got in town, Master Mark!" shouted Willie.

"Yes," replied Mark, "after I got done at the bank and you was still loading the wagon I stop by to see if it was ready but they didn't have it done yet so I came up to the store to see you. Do you remember?"

"I sure do," Willie said, "and I thank you all very much and I'll do my best to welcome your guest the way you want me to."

"Oh! now I remember Mrs. Cooper when you measured me for those work clothes, that's what it was for, wasn't it," asked Willie?

"Yes, Willie," replied Mrs. Cooper. "It was Mark's idea," she said. "Now Will and I are hoping you will represent us well when you welcome the guest into are house."

"Oh, I sure will, Mrs. Cooper, ma'am," said Willie as he took the package from Mark.

"Okay, Willie, now try the suit on to make sure it fits for Mrs. Cooper," said Will. Then he turned to Mark and said, "Let's go get dressed for church."

After Mrs. Cooper made sure the suit fit she said, "Willie, you watch for us when we come back from church and come up to the house so we can give you some practice runs before the guest start coming in. Now take the suit off and leave it here so it don't get dirty. Then you can dress when we get back," said Mrs. Cooper in a slight demanding voice.

"Okay, ma'am," said Willie as Mrs. Cooper left the room.

The Cooper's normally drove the spring wagon with all the family aboard but today Willie's dad was told to hook their finest horses to the new black buggy for Mr. and Mrs. Cooper and the spring wagon for Mark to drive with the rest of the family.

The wagon and buggy was park in fount of the big house with the slave drivers holding the lines waiting for the family to come out. When the family came out Mark took the lines so one of the slave drivers could get down and his father took the lines so the other one could get down and then they began their one hour trip to town to go to church.

Will and Mrs. Cooper arrived about 10 min or so before Mark and the kids as his father Will was showing off his new fancy buggy and high spirited horses to impress Mrs. Cooper and the towns people.

When they reached the hitching post area a crowd had already began to congregate, when a voice called out, "A mighty fine looking buggy your driving there, Will." It was the voice of Scott Lucas.

Scott looked the buggy over good, then said to Will, "Looks like the farming business is doing good this year, Will."

"Maybe we'll make enough money to pay are bills," replied Will with a slight grin.

Scott laughed and said, "Will, you farmers are all the same, you never make any money."

Will put his hand on Scott's shoulder as they walked up the path toward the church and, with a husky laugh, said, "Just trying to keep up with you big time store owners."

As they were walking up the path to church Scott said, "Did Mark tell you what happened the other day in front of my store?"

"No," replied Will, "but Willie let the cat out of the bag. Did you see the confrontation?" Will asked as he turn to look at Scott.

"No," replied Scott, "I seen a crowd gather in front of the store so I stepped out to see what was going on and that's when I seen Mark standing over Big Sean. The whole town is still talking about it."

"What's the feeling of the townspeople? Do they feel Mark was wrong?" asked Will.

"No," replied Scott, "they just all appeared shocked because Mark has always been very well-mannered and polite. But you know, Will, he does have that look in his eyes that leads one to believe that he can take care of himself."

Will smiled a little and said, "Scott, that might be the understatement of the year."

It was warm that Sunday inside the church and the front door was still open when the preacher motion to close the door as every one turn to look, there stood Big Sean Davis. It was one of the few times he had ever attended church. By now every one in the church was looking at Big Sean and looking to see if they could see Mark. They seemed to be relived when they spotted Mark up close to the front and Big Sean took a seat closer to the back.

Before he began the sermon the preacher welcome Big Sean and made mention that he hadn't seen him for a long time. The drift of the sermon that day was to love thy neighbor. Most people believed that it was directed to Big Sean and Mark. It may have been effective because as Big Sean left the church he shook the preacher's hand and then stood in the yard as if waiting for someone. His hair was still long and course looking but looked to have been recently combed. He was still wearing the pioneer-looking pants and shirt but they were clean.

The crowd would have normally dissipated soon but on this Sunday they seem to be mingling and visiting more then usual as if waiting for something to happen. Then it did happen as Mark came walking down the path to his wagon a voice called out Mark! Mark Cooper!

There stood Big Sean as he raised his large arm in motion for Mark to come over. Mark nodded his head yes as he told his brothers and sister to go down to the buggy where there parents were standing. Mark then turn back and started to walk over to where Big Sean was standing as his father Will who was standing by the buggy reached over and pulled the long black horse whip from it's holder on the buggy and started up the path behind Mark. It was common knowledge in the community that Will Cooper could pick a fly off a fence post several feet away with his long black whip. No one ever remembered him whipping his slaves but he often gave demonstration of his marksmanship to guest that would come to visit The slaves and most people in town knew how deadly accurate he could be with the whip if he had to be.

Then there came a voice from the crowd saying, "Oh My God!" Mark, by now, was just a few feet away from Big Sean when he turn to look back around to see what was going on.

His father was only ten to fifteen feet from him by now when he looked him square in the eyes and said, "I told you I'd take care of this, Dad, and expect you to honor my wishes."

"Very well," replied his father as he stood by with his whip in hand, waiting to see what was about to take place.

Mark then turned to Big Sean and said, "Okay, Sean, what do you want?"

"Well," roared Big Sean, "I could probably whip your little hind-end anytime I wanted, but it would be nice to have some skin left on my body when I got done." The roar in his voice turned into a deep laugh as he looked over at Mark's father and said, "Got yourself a fine son there, Mr. Cooper. He represents your family well." He then turn to Mark and said as he stuck out his large arm. "Son, it would be an honor to shake the hand of a boy that just turned into a man and stood up for what he believes in."

Mark stuck his hand out as the oversized hand of Big Sean's engulfed his much smaller hand. You could see in Mark's face the pain from the pressure being applied by Big Sean as he squeezed down on Mark's much smaller hand. It was during this hand shake that Mark realized how foolish it was to do what he had done to Big Sean. Mark's hand was getting numb from the pressure being applied as he thought to himself, "dad was right violence and force should be the last resort."

Big Sean was still laughing when he said, "Mark, my boy, when you get older and your dad's not standing by with that legendary whip of his, we'll have to meet again to see who the best man really is."

The feeling in Mark's hand was completely gone by now as he squeezed out a thin smile to cover the pain in his face. Big Sean being such a large man didn't look to be that tall, but Mark was over six feet tall and had to look up at him as he said, "I hope you don't think my father raised a fool."

Big Sean's laugh turned into a roar as he made one last squeeze on Mark's hand and said, "A good anser boy." When they release their hand shake Big Sean put his large arm on Mark's shoulder and said, "If your dad can spare you some time for a few months I'd like to take you with me into the wilderness land out beyond the blue ridge mountains on a hunting trip."

They both looked over at Mark's father who was by now showing a relax smile of contentment as he said to Mark, "I think your brothers and sister are ready to go home now son."

Okay, Dad," Mark replied, then he looked back up at Big Sean and said, "When you planning your next hunting trip, Sean?"

"Soon," replied Big Sean with a slight grin that had appeared between his big bushy beard.

"Maybe I'll see you in town next week some time, I've been thinking about that wilderness land ever since I read an article about it in the paper the other day," said Mark.

Both men turned and walked their separate ways; Big Sean in the direction of town and Mark in the direction of the spring wagon where his family was waiting.

As Will turn to step up into his buggy, he hesitated a moment and looked over at his son, Mark, and said, "Don't be getting any ideas of tromping into that wilderness out there with that back woodsmen. We got us a farm to take of, son."

When the wheels on their buggy and spring wagon began to roll as they left the hitching post in front of the church, you could hear voices in the crowd saying, "See you all at the party."

Chapter Four
The Secret Is Out

On the eight mile trip home Mark had a lot of time to think. Some of it was thinking how foolish he was to lash out at Big Sean the way he did. Then he realized it wasn't so much what the big man done but who he done it to. The rest of the way home Mark's mind was pondering with the thought of what he would have to do if it became public knowledge that Willie could read.

When the Cooper family arrived in front of the big house the slaves took the lines from Mark and his father so they could go on up to the house then they drove the wagon and buggy off to put them away.

Willie received the family at the front door in his slave clothes saying, "Welcome to the Cooper home, and may I ask who's calling, ma'am?"

Mrs. Cooper looked at Willie with a little grin and said, "Willie's Boss."

"They have been expecting you, ma'am," said Willie as he held the door open so they could enter. Willie then topped it off by saying, "May I take your wrap, ma'am?"

"Yes, Willie," she replied, "and tell Ann I'm home."

"I sure will, ma'am," said Willie with a big old smile that seemed to light up the room. "Did I do a good job, ma'am?"

"Yes, Willie," said Mrs. Cooper but we still have to polish your technique so go and change now and be back in about half hour." When Willie left the room to tell Ann that Mrs. Cooper was back all the kids were following him laughing and saying, "May I take your wrap, Mrs. Cooper, ma'am?"

Ann entered the room shortly and said, "Willie said you wanted to talk to me, ma'am."

"How are the cooks doing with the meal?" asked Mrs. Cooper, "and will it be ready by two o'clock?"

"I just talk to them, ma'am, and they assured me it would be ready to serve on time and it does smell and taste good," answered Ann with a mischievous smile.

"Oh, you been doing the boss's job have you," said Mrs. Cooper as she smiled and winked at her. "Ann," she said, "you can tell the cooks I'll be in to check with them shortly. In the meantime you begin setting the tables."

"Okay," replied Ann as she left the room.

Mrs. Cooper had the slaves to set up the tables while they were in church. The big formal dining room would set up to twenty people, the family dining that they used daily would seat twelve normally but with the add table would seat twenty four.

An older slave named Tom was normally used to greet the guest when they had parties and special events, but Mark had asked his mother and father to allow Willie to do it this year for his birthday.

Willie was now dressed as he went to the kitchen to see Mrs. Cooper. "How do I look, Mrs. Cooper, ma'am?" asked Willie with a big smile.

"You look fine, Willie, now let's go and do some practice runs," replied Mrs. Cooper.

As they left the kitchen she motion for Tom to come along. Tom wasn't there to receive guest but there to help give Willie some pointers. Before they began the practice runs Mrs. Cooper showed Willie the guest list on a little table to the left of the front door.

Now she said, "The names of the guests are listed here, so when the guests knock on the door hold it open until they have entered into the house. Then you say, 'Welcome to the Cooper's home. May I ask who's calling, please.' Then you say, 'Just a moment, please,' and come into the reception room where either I, Mr. Cooper, or Mark will be standing by. Then whoever comes to receive the guest will draw a line through the name on the guest list."

"Now," she said as she looked at Tom, "you go outside and knock on the door."

"Willie, you do what I told you to and I'll be standing at the door in the reception room. Now talk loud enough that I can hear you as I want to make sure you are doing it right."

They did three or four more practice runs then Mrs. Cooper seemed satisfied she said now, "Willie, when the guests have left the room you stand by the guest list table. I don't want you wandering all around the house, interfering with the guests."

"Okay," said Willie as he walked over and stood by the guest list table.

Mrs. Cooper started to leave the room when she turned to Willie and asked, "Willie, do you get a sandwich like I told you to from the kitchen?"

"Yes, ma'am," replied Willie with a smaller smile than normal.

Mrs. Cooper noticed Willie was a little nervous and said with a little wink from her eye, "You'll do just fine, Willie, just do what I told you to do and be yourself. The guest will be coming soon so good luck, Willie." She then turned and left the room.

Willie looked at the guest list and realized he knew a few of the names but there were several he didn't know. Mrs. Cooper was right, as the first knock came at the door shortly after she left. Willie greeted the guest the way he was told and when Mrs. Cooper came in to receive them she walked over and drew a line through their name. This is as easy as falling off a log Willie thought to himself as he walked back over to the guest list.

The house was starting to fill up when there came a knock on the door Willie opened the door and greeted them the same as usual but this time Mrs. Cooper wasn't there so he told Mr. Cooper the name of the guest. He came in to greet them but didn't draw a line through the name on the list. As they were leaving the room Mr. Cooper realized he hadn't drew a line through the name.

He was talking to Mr. Bill Brown a well to do farmer in the neighborhood when he called back to Willie and said, "Cross off the Browns, Willie."

He was so engrossed in his conversation with Mr. Brown he forgot about Willie not knowing how to read.

"Yes sir master Will," replied Willie as he looked for the name Brown.

Mr. Cooper said to Mr. Brown, "You know Ann gets upset when I don't greet the guest properly."

"Yes, I know, Will, but I didn't know you had any slaves that could read."

"I don't," replied Will as he hesitated then turn to look back to Willie.

There was Willie leaning over the guest list drawing a line through a name. Will looked to be in a state of shock as he and Bill walked over to Willie and the guest list. Mark was just entering the room to see how Willie was doing. When his father Will said to Willie in a loud and demanding voice after he had seen the name Brown with a line drawn through it. "How did you know where to draw that line Willie?"

Willie's eyes were double their size by now as he realized what a terrible mistake he had made. "I just," he started to say, "guest at it," when Mark called out, "No, Willie!"

Will by now realized he had asked Willie to do something he shouldn't be able to do.

"Willie!" Mark said in a commanding, stern voice. "It's time you tell my father the whole truth and nothing but the truth, that means everything. Do you Understand?"

"Yes, sir, Master Mark. Master Will, sir, I's learn to read when I was little and I know now that the law forbids it, so if you have to use that whip on me I'll understand." He then looked back over at Mark as if to say, "I can't tell him you taught me."

"Now wait a minute, Willie," demanded Will, "you didn't learn to read by yourself so I want to know who taught you."

Mark started to say something when Willie shouted to override his voice, "Master Will, sir, I will not tell you who taught me how to read. I have the greatest respect for you, sir, so if you must whip or sell me or both I will understand. Master Will, sir," he said as he lowered his voice, "I also want you to know that my mom and dad do not know that I can read."

Will looked at Willie in complete dismay and said, "There will be no whipping on the Lord's day, but I'll expect you to be at the big tree out back when you are called to go to work in the morning."

Mark, by now, had reached Willie's side as he looked at his father with cold black eyes that seemed to penetrate his father's eyes like daggers going through hot melted metal. He then said to his father, "And the first crack of that whip shall be upon my back for I am the one who taught Willie to read and I knew it was against your will! You have told me many times that when we have a problem force and violence should be the last resort. Well, Father, we have a problem, the three of us, and one thing I know for sure is Willie is not the source of the problem!"

Mrs. Cooper and some of the other guest had heard the demanding voice's of Mark, Willie and Will and came in to see what was going on. By this time the controlled sound of Will Cooper's voice had turned into a violent roar as he said to Mark, "One more outburst from you, son, and I won't wait till tomorrow to use that whip!"

"That will be enough!" shouted Mrs. Cooper at the top of her lungs. There were tears rolling down her cheeks as she said, "There will be no more talk of whipping on the Lord's day! This matter will be settled tomorrow in the presence of our family only and not in the present of the community."

"Willie," she said in a demanding voice, "you stay by the door as there is still a few guests coming and have them come on into the dining room." She then said to her guest, "If you will follow me to the dining room, please."

As ever one began to set at their assigned sets there was complete silence not even Will or Mark said a word. In a few minutes Willie brought the rest of the guest in. When they were seated Mrs. Cooper said I have an announcement to make. "I apologize for myself and family for the bar room behavior at the fount door. Please keep on socializing with each other and remember a good party needs an ample amount of laughter." She then motioned for Ann to begin serving as she said, "Dinner will now be served."

Chapter Five
The Temptation of an Apple

The dinner went well, considering the tension that was noticeable between Mark and his father, they didn't talk but their eyes did come in contact with each other a few times. There was normal laughter and conversation by the time the meal was over. Even Mark and his father caught there selves talking and laughing with the guest. One of the conversation that came up, was how Mark's horse got the name Apple Bee.

The dinner was coming to an end when Will stood up and said, "Gentleman, it's time to let the races begin, so bring your fastest horse down by the big tree so we can get this race started."

Mrs. Cooper stood up and said, "Now don't forget to be back here in an hour for cake and desert."

As the men began to leave the room a voice called out, "does this mean you won't be demonstrating that fancy whip of yours to day Will."

"It sure does," replied Will as he looked at Mrs. Cooper with a small grin.

As the men were leaving the room Scott Locus turn to Mark and asked, "Are you going to run your horse today, Mark?"

Mark looked at his father as if to say, *I don't know*.

Then his father looked back at him and said, "Of course, he's going to run. We can't let those city horses out run them county horses now can we, Scott."

Mark's father had given Mark a horse for his nineteenth birthday and he won the race last year on his twentieth birthday so every one was going to try to beat him this year. You could see all the men that was going to run their horses was worried because they new Mark was an expert horsemen and was a fierce competitor. Mark then rose from his chair and decided to check on Willie as he felt partly responsible for the trouble he was in. As he looked into the reception room that was now empty he saw Willie standing by the door eating an apple. His thin smile turned into a large grin as he said, "Wish me luck, Willie."

Willie raised his large arm up that was holding the apple that had a bit taken out of it and said, "I sure will, Master Mark, sir.

The men that weren't in the race were on the finish line waiting to see who the winner would be. Some of the slaves were helping in the race and the rest were beyond the finish line waiting and watching with out blocking the view of the guest.

The front porch by now was filled with some of the women who were watching but trying not to look over anxious. One of course was Mrs. Cooper. Willie had asked Mrs. Cooper if he could watch and she said, "Yes, but stand at the other end of the porch out of everyone's way." Mark was getting his horse ready for the race when he looked up and saw Willie standing on the fount porch.

He then looked at his father and said, "I'm going to warm Apple Bee up and I'll be right back." Apple Bee was the name he gave his horse when he saw Willie give him a apple with a bee on it soon after his father gave him to Mark.

Mark rode up to the porch and said, "Mother, will you have Willie go get an apple and bring it down to the open area just in back of the finish line."

His mother smiled a little and said, "Okay, Mark." His mother knew what Mark was up to so she told Willie to take the apple that was in her lap down to Mark in back of the finish line.

When Mrs Cooper handed Willie the apple Willie started to grin and said, "I sure will, Mrs. Cooper, ma'am."

When Willie got down to where Mark was, he was sitting on Apple Bee getting ready to start the race.

He looked down at Willie and said, "I just asked Dad if you could watch the race from here and he said okay, but stay out of everyone's way. So give Apple Bee a bite of the apple and stay back out of the way until I start around that last corner then hold the apple up over your head until I cross the finish line."

Willie's eyes were getting larger as his grin turned into a laugh he said, "Yes, sir, Master Mark, sir!"

Every one by now was over at the starting line and wasn't aware of Mark and Willie over a the finish line. Mark rode over and took his spot in the starting line just in time for the race to start. His father's left hand went up to give the ready signal in his other hand was his long black whip. A few seconds passed and then his left hand came down and his right hand came up and down so quick that the sound of the whip as it snapped sounded like a gun firing with a double load in it.

The race was on and the horses was about 50 yards out in just a few seconds. By the time they were about 100 yards out Apple Bee was in third place. They disappeared behind the barn and buildings for a time, then when they reappeared Apple Bee was in second place behind Joe Conklin, the son of James Conklin that owned the mill in town.

James Colin looked over at Mark's father and said with a little grin, "Will, it looks like the city boys are about to show the county boys a thing or two about horsemanship."

By this time Joe Conklin was whipping his horse violently coming into the back stretch to the finish line. Mark didn't believe in whipping a horse to win a race. He believed you could get the most from your horse by being a good master and knowing your horse as well as yourself.

Mark was leaning over as if to be saying something to Apple Bee when his father replied to Mr. Conklin's remark by saying, "James, it's best you don't laugh until your funny bone has been tickled." About that time Mark's hand went up in the air to signal Willie to hold the apple up. When Willie's hand went up with the apple in it Apple Bee shot forward like a lead ball coming out of the barrow of a gun. Apple Bee and Mark crossed the finish line a good half length a head of Joe Colin who by now had stopped the violent whipping of his horse, Dream Buster.

Apple Bee took a bite of the apple Willie was holding and shook his head in contentment as Mark swung down and said, "Good job, Willie."

All the men that didn't have a horse in the race laughed at what they had just seen take place.

Will Cooper was laughing as he slapped Mr. Conklin on the back and said, "I guess one shouldn't count their chickens until they hatch should they James?"

James replied back with a slight bit of resentment as he answered by saying, "an one should watch their apples for one bad one can spoil the hold bunch."

Will's smile turned to a serious look as he thought about what he had to do tomorrow.

When James who was called Jim by every one seen the serious look on Will's face he said as he put his hand out, "I'm sorry, Will, that was unfair of me to say that. I know Willie is a good boy and I know it's going to be hard for you to do what you have to do tomorrow." Jim reached out to shake Will's hand and said, "Mark ran a good race and I guess he showed a lot of us that the temptation of an apple is greater than the bite of a whip."

With a serious look still on his face, Will answered him by saying, "Yes, I guess he did run a good race, Jim. But that boy is constantly forcing me to doubt what I used to except as right and wrong."

Jim thought a little bit and said, "You know, Will, maybe the passing of time does change our sense of right and wrong."

"Could be," replied Will as they walked over to congratulate Mark.

As they were approaching Mark, Joe Conklin rode up to Mark and said, "Congratulations on your win. I guess you salt and pepper boys have been practicing that underhanded trick for a long time, haven't you?"

Mark's black eyes snapped as he glared up at Joe and said, "Probably not as long as you have been practicing your barbaric whipping technique that don't appear to be working."

"Now, gentlemen," shouted Will, "don't be acting like boys. Them days are over. Mark, you got a farm to run someday and Joe you got a mill to run someday so your friendship may determine your success."

"Amen, to that," replied Jim to Will's remark.

Joe stepped down from his horse and shook Mark's hand as he said, "I guess the old folks are right again."

Mark replied by saying, "Maybe they didn't hear the old folks part of that statement."

They both were laughing as they walked away with their horses.

Chapter Six
Love at First Sight

The dinner bell began to ring as everyone left for the big house to get some desert. Mark was the last to leave the barn and as he walked back to the house he was thinking how his mother stood up to his father that no man dare to talk back to. He also remembered the times she showed compassion for his feelings by allowing him to be master of his house. As he reach for the knob to the back door, he said to himself, "Will I ever find the right one that was made just for me like my father did?" Little did he know at that moment in time that his life was about to change forever.

Willie was standing in the front room when a knock on the front door sounded. He answered the door as usual just as Mark stepped into the room to check on him. Willie told Mark who the guess was. Mark then walk over and welcome the Howiton family.

"There was a rumor in the area at the time that Mrs. Howiton was related to Benedick Arnold the traitor."

Mark took them over to the dining room where they met Mrs. Cooper and Mr. Howiton apologized for being late.

They were taking their seats when Mark noticed that their daughter had went from a skinny little girl to a gorgeous young lady from the time he seen her last. Ann and some kitchen help brought the cake in and lit the twenty-one candles. Then when Mark went to blow out the candles everyone sang happy birthday to him.

When everyone was done with their desert and had started visiting, Mark went over to Sarah Howiton and said, "Sarah, you haven't seen my horse yet, have you?"

"No, I haven't," she replied.

Mark grinned a little and said, "Would you like to walk with me out to see him?"

She smiled back at him and said, "I can't wait."

Mark's hart was pounding as he was searching for the right words to say to her.

She must have sensed his nerviness, for as she got up to go with him, she said, "Mark, I overheard someone saying you won the race. Is that right?"

"Yes, I guess I was pretty lucky," he replied.

She smiled and said, "That's not what I heard. I heard that you were the apple of everyone's eye."

Mark replied by saying, "You know people have a way of making more out of something than it really is."

"Oh," she said, "I like that not only are you compassionate, you're modest, too," as she swung her head back to allow her long blond hair to flow in the breeze of the afternoon sun.

Mark turned to look at her as his black snappy eyes came in contact with her beep blue eyes, causing an attraction that was so strong that it appeared to be pulling two worlds together to form one. Even back then this was commonly known as love at first sight. The pounding in Mark's hart became more rapid when he caught himself holding her long blond hair in his hands as the afternoon breezes blew it gently through his fingers. Her hart was fluttering like the wings of a hummingbird in pursuit of a brilliant red flower.

She then put her hands on his big broad shoulders and, at the same time, they both said, "We best go see that horse now."

They began to walk to the barn when she through her head in a way to allow her hair to blow in the air again as she said, "The last one to the barn is a rotten apple."

IN SEARCH OF FREE LAND

Mark stood for a few seconds as he watched her long, sleek legs carry a swirling dress that rapped around her showing the extreme curvature of her well-developed body. Her dress blowing in the wind as she ran left little for the imagination as Mark caught himself running at full speed to catch her.

At the barn door she turned, still laughing, and started to say, "Rotten apple," when Mark's hand went up against the barn as if to hold her from getting away.

He then moved his lips close to hers ever so gently, so as not to cross a boundary that may be off limits to him. She moved her arms around his slender waist as she felt his powerful body pull her in and then she surrendered to his command. With their bodies locked together and the passion flowing like water going down a roaring river the sound of the real world seemed to dissipate as Mark caught himself surrendering to her desires. He then released his arms from around her body and pushed out from the barn to allow her to be free to move.

With her arms still locked around his body Mark said to her as he looked into her deep blue eyes, "We must delay our passion today. Now that you know as well as I do, that it will take a lifetime to tame our desires for each other."

Before she loosened her arms from around his body she looked up into his pitch black eyes smiled and replied, "No, Mark. It's going to take more than a life time. Its going to take generations to calm the flow of our passion for each other."

Mark looked at her smiled and said, "Does that mean we are going to have a lot of children?"

"It sure does," she said as she took his hand and walked with him back toward the house.

About halfway to the house there was a bench beside a water tank. Mark stopped and asked her if she would sit and talk with him.

She replied, "I'm going to be talking to you forever so why not start now."

"Sarah," he said as he looked at her in a concerned way. "I've got some big problems," he started to say.

But before he could go on she put her finger on his lips and said,

"No, honey, we have some big problem. You remember all that passion we were just experiencing down at the barn, well that goes for our problems as well."

"Do you know our slave, Willie?" Mark asked.

"Yes, I've heard of him."

"Well, I taught him to read when we were young and no one knew about it until today. Now that other slave owners know about it my father will have no choice but to take the whip to him tomorrow and maybe even sale him off to another owner far from here."

She looked at Mark with a serious look on her face as she said, "Mark, I've heard my mother and father talk about you and Willie when I was growing up as a child. They said you were always doing things together and they sensed a friendship forming between you. They also was concerned about what would happen when you got old enough to become a part of the decision making process on the farm."

"Well," Mark said, "that time has come, but I'm not really ready for it yet because, you see, I don't really believe in slavery."

"I understand," he said in a hesitant way as if to be asking for her help, "that it is the way of life here and I know how important it is that they don't lean to read. But now that he can, do to no fault of his own, should he be denied the hopes and dreams that may be unveiled to him between the covers of a book?"

Sarah ran her fingers through his black, wavy hair as she said with a little smile, "It's too complicated for me, but I'm sure you will do what you have to when the time comes." As they stood up, she added, "Like you did with that Big Sean Davis guy."

"Oh, you heard about that, did you?"

"I think about everyone has by now, Mark."

They started in the direction of the house when Mark said, "You didn't get to see my horse."

"Who's fault was that," she said as she swung her hair to the side and looked up at him with a mischievous smile.

"The next time I promise we'll go in the barn and see Apple Bee," Mark said as he reached around her shoulders and pulled her in close to him.

She cuddled up to him as they walked away and said, "I double dare you!"

As they entered the house some of the guess were getting ready to leave and Willie was standing by to escort them to the door. Before anyone left the house Will Cooper asked everyone to gather in the reception room for a short announcement.

"It saddens me," he said, "to have to make this announcement on the Lord's day. We just found out today that one of our slaves has broken the law of the land by learning to read and one of our family has participated in allowing it to happen. So to protect the investment of all the slave owners we have no choice but to enforce justes according to the law that we have come to live by, be it right or be it wrong. For those of you who have slaves that you feel need to witness this, feel free to bring them. But I asked you please do not come just to watch. The punishment will begin in the morning down at the big tree in the back yard at 9:00 sharp."

The word sharp was still ringing in the air when Mark held his arm high above everyone and said, "And I will be delivering the fifty lashes as prescribed for this particular offence. Then after Willie has been cut down from the tree and the wounds attended to, my father will make the decision as to what my punishment must be."

"Mark," his father said in a stern voice, "tell the people how old you were when you taught Willie to read.

"Well I guess I must have been about 8 years old.

Mark's father had made his point to his guess, he wanted them to here from Mark's voice how old he was when he taught Willie to read. He thought to him self before he asked the question, "Mark probably taught Willie to read at a yong age as he was a very good reader when he was young. If this is true, he thought that the community would feel less harsh toward him."

In the early 1800s the slave owners in the state of Virginia didn't take it lightly when someone taught a slave to read because it could devalue their investment so Mark's father was trying to ease the tension while he decided what he would have to do.

Mark held his hand up again as he said, "I thank each of you for the gifts that you gave me and I apologize for the injustice that I may have injected not only to my family but to the community as well."

As guess began to leave Mrs. Cooper was at the door to thank each and everyone personally for coming to the party. Willie's normally big smile had turned to a small grin as he opened and closed the door for the guess to leave. The Howiton Family was among the last ones to leave. They were talking to Mrs. Cooper as Sarah and Mark came into the room behind them and stood a few steps from where Willie was standing. Sarah looked at Mark and Willie at same time as she seen their eyes meet and thought to herself of what a terrible day they both would have tomorrow. She then said to them, "What an awful price you both have to pay tomorrow for such a simple thing as reading."

"Oh no, ma'am," Willie replied, "there's no price short of death that's too high for the joys that I've received from what Mark taught me when we were little kids."

Mark rubbed Willie's kinky black hair with his hand as he said with a little grin, "Willie, you better go open the door for Mr. and Mrs. Howiton."

"Yes, sir, Master Mark, sir."

Sarah new by now that the bond that this master and his slave had formed could not be broken by the mere fifty lashes of a long black whip. She then went over still holding Mark's hand and told Mrs. Cooper how nice the party was.

Mrs. Cooper looked at both of them smiled and said, "Looks like Mark's done well on his birthday."

Sarah put her arms around Mrs. Cooper and said, "I hope he got everything he wanted."

Mrs. Cooper, still smiling, replied back, "I'm sure he did!"

Sarah looked at Mark as if to say, "Aren't you going to hug me before I leave."

Mark sensed the invitation and put his arm around her as her mother and father watched while standing at the door, waiting for Sarah.

"Sarah," Mark said with a concerned look on his face, "I may be going out west in a few days on a hunting trip, but before I go I would

IN SEARCH OF FREE LAND

like to come to your house to see you if that's okay with your mother and father."

Both Mr. and Mrs. Howiton replied at the same time, "Of course that's okay, but plan on having dinner with us."

"I will," said Mark as they turned and walked outside. "I'll see you to the buggy," Mark said to Sarah as he took her hand and followed Mr. and Mrs. Howiton out.

Willie closed the door behind them as Mrs. Cooper started into the other room. "Will you be needing me anymore today, Mrs. Cooper, ma'am?" Willie asked.

She was walking into the other room by now and seen that only Jim Conklin and Scott Lucas were left talking to Mr. Cooper.

She replied to Willie by saying, "No, Willie, you can go on home now, but change your clothes before you leave." With a troubled look on her face, she said, "Maybe you better wait after you change your clothes for Mr. Conklin and Mr. Lucas to leave in case Mr. Cooper wants to talk to you."

"Okay, ma'am," Willie said as he left to change his clothes. Willie sensed Mrs. Cooper's troubled look turn and said, before he left the room, "I'll be okay, ma'am, and I want you to know I'll always love this family, regardless of what has to be done to me."

A tear was rolling down Mrs. Cooper's cheek as she said, "May God be with you, Willie."

The Conklin and Lucas family were walking out to their buggies as Mark was waving goodbye to Sarah.

He had turned to the Lucas and Conklin family as Joe Conklin said, "Looks like you got yourself a nice surprise birthday gift there, Mark."

Mark grinned and replied by saying, "Well she's not really a gift as she don't belong to me, but I do admit she was a surprise to me. But you know all about them surprises, too, don't you, Joe."

They all laughed and said their goodbyes as Mark turned to walk up to the house where his father was standing there watching. His father appeared to be in deep thought as Mark walk by him into the house. Will had already told Willie to go on home and Mrs. Cooper had done excused Ann for the evening. She also sent the kids with Ann so

47

they could play with some of the slave kids for an hour or two. Mrs. Cooper new that the time had come for Mark and his father to talk about the dreaded decision that would have to be made and implemented tomorrow.

When he entered the house Mark's father said, "It's time to go to the family dining room and get started," as he walked by Mrs. Cooper and Mark.

When they all sat down at the table Will said to Mrs. Cooper, "Ann, will you bring us some coffee?"

She pushed her chair back as she stood up and said, "Only if you both act civilized and don't use barbaric language."

They both nodded their head in agreement as she left the room.

In a demanding tone Will said to his son, "Mark, why in God's name didn't you tell me about this when you got old enough to know that we can't condone it?"

Mark looked at his father for a moment in silence and then said, "Dad, it's hard to explain. I guess by the time I got old enough to know that it was wrong in your eyes it seemed right in my eyes. So the older I got the harder it became to tell you about it."

"Son, let me ask you a question," his father said. "Suppose that Apple Bee that you like so much got out and ended up in an area where there's not enough food and water plus the constant chance of being attacked by bears. Would it be better to leave him there to survive the best he could or would it be better to bring him home so you could protected him?"

"I see your point, Dad," Mark paused then went on to say, "It's not that I am so against slavery if they are treaded properly, but I guess I am against them not having the opportunity to read if they have that burning desire and a God given ability like Willie has."

"Dad," he said in a higher tone of voice, "Willie was able to read fluently by the time he was 10 years old! Yet how many times has he tried to run away?"

"What are you try to say, Mark?" asked his father as he got up and walked around the table in deep thought.

Mark thought for a short time then he said to his father, "Dad, I don't think it would be wise to have twenty Willies working for you, but I do think you are extremely fortunate to have one. I believe one Willie-type slave handled properly would offer hope to the other slaves and, Dad, I believe that hope is a condition for life for all people, be they slave or free."

Mrs. Cooper was just coming in with the coffee when Will looked at his son in a troubled way and said, "Mark, do you think Willie has or ever had the desire to run away to see if the grass is greener on the other side of the fence?"

"Yes," Mark replied to his father's question, "there's no doubt about it. The fact he can read has stirred a burning desire in him to be free to go see what's on the other side of the blue ridge. In fact dad I've got a desire to go west and it comes from what I've read about it, but I known I have an obligation here to you and the family. There's one difference between Willie's situation and mind and that is I'm free to make that choice but Willie only has hope that you someday may allow him to go look at that sun set on the other side of the blue ridge."

"It appears were not making it any easier talking about it, the fact still remains I have to put fifty lashes on Willie's back tomorrow morning," said Mark's father as he took a sip of coffee that Mrs. Cooper had brought.

Mark took a sip of his coffee and said, "No, Dad, I'm the one who has to put the whip to Willie's back. You didn't teach him to read, I did."

His father look at him with compassion and said, "No, son, you was just a child when it happened so I can't hold you responsible for teaching him, but I do hold you responsible for failing to tell me when you got old enough to know that it was against my will."

Mark took another sip of coffee and said, "Dad, I think I have a solution to our problem."

"Okay, let's hear it," said his father with an uninterested facial expression.

Mark answered by saying, "Instead of giving Willie fifty lashes, give him twenty-five and give me twenty-five, then sign a note with me down at the bank so I can buy Willie from you."

"That's the silliest damn thing I've ever heard. No one is expected to whip their own son for teaching a slave to read when he was too young to know what he was doing," replied his father.

"I know, Dad, but please hear me out," said Mark as he took another sip of coffee. He then went on to say, "If you was to loan me enough money to buy Willie and give us a six months leave from the farm we could take that trip out west. Who knows maybe it would end up benefitting you as well as satisfying our desire to see that sunset on the other side of the blue ridge. From what I've read there're lots of opportunities out there if you got the grit to challenge the unknown."

"Son," his father said, "you got to have some sort of plan, you can't just take off into the wilderness with a starry-eyed slave tagging alone behind you."

"I do have a plan, Dad," replied Mark, "I intend to join up with Big Sean Davis. His goals may be different than mine, but he may have the expertise to allow me to pursue my goals, which may, in turn, be a benefit to you. Who knows, Dad. Willie may end up a needed commodity to all of us."

His father grinned a little and said, "Son, you're talking about land, aren't you?"

Mark's black eye's were dancing as he grinned and said, "Yes, Dad, especially if it's free land!"

His father started to say something when Mrs. Cooper interrupted by saying, "Before this goes too far, due what you must to solve this problem, but I will not tolerate you taken that whip to our son, Will Cooper!"

"Okay, Ann," he said to her, "you have my word on that."

She went on to say, "I have never interfered with your decision on matters such as this, but I do think you should consider very carefully what Mark has to say."

He looked at his wife Ann, winked his eye and said, "You know, Mom, it would solve a lot of our problems." He thought for a bit and went on to say, "I wouldn't have to take Willie to another part of the county to sell him." A serious look had returned to his face as he said to her, "Ann, the hard part is I still have to put those fifty lashes on Willie's back."

Ann sensed the torment that her husband Will was going through trying to come to grip with what he had to do. She then got up waked over behind his chair put her arms around his shoulders and said, "Will Cooper, I've seen you take a fly off of an apple and never break the skin with that whip of yours. I also know all that practicing you been doing over the years and the demonstration you've been putting on was not just to scare the slaves even tho it has worked very well. It has allowed you the expertise to apply the punishment if ever needed with the minium amount of pain."

Mark spoke out and said, "Dad, that was your way of fighting the system that as come to be a guide for us to live by, isn't it?"

His father looked at him, hesitated before he spoke, then said, "Or maybe I was trying to make sure it worked the way it was supposed to."

"Speaking of how things are supposed to work, how in the world do you think we can run this place if you go tromping off out through the Cumberland Gap with that mountain man."

"Dad, do we really have a choice?" Mark replied to his father's comment. He went on to say, "And there's still the issue of what my punishment will be."

His father forced a little laugh from his worried looking face and said, "Well, son, I believe six months out in the back woods country with a roaring mountain man and a starry-eyed slave boy might be more than enough punishment for this so called crime you committed."

Mark relied with a gleam in his eye as he said, "Does that mean I can go, Dad?"

His father saw that sparkle in his eyes and thought to himself, *He's going with or without my consent*, and said, "If that's okay with your mother, then go with our blessing, but make damn sure you're back here in six months!"

"Will Cooper," Ann said to her husband, "watch your language. You know it's still the Lord's day."

"Okay, Ann," Will replied as he got up from his chair and said, "Mark, make sure you take care of Willie because after today he will be your property."

Mark was getting up from his chair when he seen the sad look on his father's face, he then turn to face his father and said, "You can count on me, Dad."

His father walked over, stood by his mother, put his arm around her shoulder and said, "We know we can, son."

"I have to go to the office and do some work now so I'll see you in the morning for breakfast." He started to leave when he turned back to Mark and said, "After we attend to Willie wound's you and I will be going to the bank in town to transfer the ownership of Willie over to you."

When Mark's father left the room his mother came over to Mark and put her arms around him and said, "Oh, how I hate to see you leave, but I know the time has come for you to go out and experience some of your own dreams. Hopefully, then you'll come back to fulfill your father's dreams that he has for you, not to just run the farm, but help him to build the Cooper plantation."

Mark's black eyes looked deep into his mother's pal blue eye's as he said, "Mom, my dad is a tough act to follow, but I'll do my best to make you both proud of me." He gave her a kiss on the cheek, smiled and said, "I hope you and Dad both like the idea of being grandpa and grandma because Sarah and I plan on being highly productive in this area."

His mother wiggled out a small grin from the concerned look on her face as she said, "Make sure you prepare the groundwork well before you start planting any seeds."

"Mother," Mark said, "your point is well taken and I might add very good advise but when you have been fortunate enough to experience love at first sight nothing else ready matters."

His mother smiled and said, "Looks like you been bit by that old love bug. Now you have to be careful because sometimes after you've been bit you start to hallucinate and see things that's not ready there."

"Mother," he replied with a smile, "I think you're right because I can see Sarah now as plain as day in my mind's eye with all those kids riding with me over to there Grandpa and Grandma's house for Sunday dinner."

She looked at Mark with her pale blue eyes, smiled and said, "Mark, are you trying to manipulate your mother?"

Mark laughed and said, "I guess so, Mom."

She winked and said, "You may have done it with that grandpa and grandma part." As she left the room she turned and said, "Oh, by the way, I do like Sarah. She seems like a very nice young lady."

After his mother left the room Mark walked over to the dining room window and looked out toward the west where the sitting sun was moving downward giving off a red glare alone the horizon. That glare was so bright that it reflected back into the office and onto the desk of Will Cooper, at the same time it found it's way to peak through an open window in a tinny slave cabin where Willie was laying on his bed looking up at the ceiling. With his hands together and looking down at the light on his desk Will asked the Lord to forgive him for what he was about to do tomorrow. At the same moment in time Willie got up walked over to the window and as he looked at the setting sun. The view that was reflected back into the eyes of Mark and Willie crossed some where west beyond the blue ridge. Their minds began to paint a picture to them, a view of the legendary Cumberland Gap trail through the mountains and on west to the Kentucky Country. The sun moved on down and out of sight as darkness fall upon the Cooper family and their slaves.

Another Sunday had passed away as the Lords day came to an end with the silent sound of Will Cooper saying, "Amen."

Chapter Seven
Willie's Punishment

From out of the east there was a light forming on the horizon just as the old rooster step out of the hen house and made sure all was up for the day. You could here the sound of the slave cabin doors opening and closing and the smoke coming out of the chimneys as the rising sun rose above the earth. After their morning choirs was done and breakfast served the slaves began to gather around the big tree in the back yard of the big house. By now of all of the slaves new about what was going to happen, even Willie's Mom and Dad. There was a few wagons coming down the road from the neighboring plantation and farms bringing some of their slaves to witness the occasion. Willie's Mom and Dad and family including Willie were the last one's to come out of the cabins. As they walked up to the tree every one was waiting and watching when they walked by. Willie's Mom was crying as Willie and his Dad held on to her. The rest of the kids were following behind. The first person to come out of the Cooper house was Mark as he walked down and told Willie to go in the house to see his father. Mark then held Willie's Mom's arm as Willie left. Mrs. Cooper would not allow the rest of her family to go out side. When Willie stepped inside the house his master Will was standing at the door.

He told Willie to close the door, then he said, "Willie, listen to me very carefully. Mark will be trying you to the tree but he will leave the rope a little loose so back away from the tree to keep the rope tight. Now when you hear the swishing sound of the whip in the air you say to yourself one and hug that tree as tight as you can. This will allow your body to go in and out a few inches from the tree. I will be attempting to crack the whip at the right time to prevent to much damage to your back. After you feel the bit of the whip push back from the tree to tighten up the rope, then when you hear the swishing sound of the whip again say one and hug that tree with all you might." Will rubbed his hand through Willie's kinky hair and said, "Willie, this will be the last day you belong to me. Starting tomorrow Mark will be your new owner. Mark will be taken you out west with him so you'll get a change to see what freedom is all about. So Willie, every time you hear the swishing sound of the whip, hug that tree as tight as you can and think about that trip to freedom. Maybe it will help."

"Now," Will said, "you go on out and I'll be right behind you."

Willie opened the door and started out when his master said, "Willie, will you do me a favor before you and Mark leave for out west?"

"Yes," replied Willie as he turned back to face his master.

"Stop by my office sometime and read me one of those stories you learned when you were little."

Willie grinned with a tear in his eyes and said, "I sure will, Master Will, sir," and then he turned and walked out to the big tree.

Mark was tying Willie to the tree when Willie said, "Master Mark, sir, will you bring the book that you taught me to read from down to my cabin when this over?"

"Yes, Willie, I will, now remember every time you hear the swishing sound of that whip give that tree a big bear hug!"

Willie leaned back as Mark step away and in just a few seconds he heard the first swishing sound of the whip as he said to himself, "One," and hugged that tree with all his might. Then came the sting on his back, by the time he heard the next sound of the whip he felt a bitting pain. After about the third whip Willie noticed there was less pain and he thought to himself, *Oh My God I'm going to make it!*

Even tho it was hurting and he knew there was blood on his back he felt the mercy at the end of that whip and for the first time realized why his master had practice so much and put on so many demonstration. Now he knew his master was handling his legendary whip like a great artist drawing a famous picture. Even tho he couldn't see his master he knew there was tears in his eyes each time the long black whip make a cracking sound and he thought to himself, *My back will heal soon, but the scar left on his heart will probably never heal completely.*

The tears were rolling down the cheeks of Will and Willie both as Willie said, "May god have mercy on his soul!" Willie had lost track of the number of times the whip cracked, but still had enough strength to pull his body back and forth to ease the pain.

Then came the silence of the whip as Willie heard the sweetest words ever spoken when his master said, "Cut him down."

Will turned and walked back to the house as Mark cut the rope.

Mark looked at the blood oozing from Willie's black shinny back and in a compassionate tone to his voice he asked, "Can you walk, Willie?"

"Yes, I think so," replied Willie as the tears of pain and pity rolled down his rounded cheeks.

Mark then helped Willie over to a bench near by. The door on the big house opened as Ann, Willie's sister came running out with a wash pan full of water, soap and some lotion to rub on his back.

Ann asked, "Is he going to be okay, Mark."

"Yes, Annie, he'll be okay in a few days you just keep his back clean and keep putting the lotion on a couple of times a day." After he was treaded his family all helped to walk him back to their cabin as Mark went back into his house.

The rest of the slaves had all went back to work by now and the neighbors had left too. Mark found the book Willie had asked for and took it down to the cabin. Willie didn't know it but Mark had put an article about Daniel Boone inside the book. Willie seen the article and was reading it to his family when Mark opened the door to leave. He hesitated at the door of the little cabin for a moment as he heard him read to them the words, "there are hundreds of people going across the mountains beyond the blue ridge by means of a trail called the Cumberland Gap." Willie stopped reading and said, "Guess what, Mom? Mark's my new owner now and he's taking me with him out through the Cap to a place called Kentucky!"

Mark stepped away from the door as he shook his head, grinned, and thought to himself, *My father might be right about me going out west with a roaring mountain man and a starry-eyed slave boy.*

Chapter Eight
Planning for the Big Trip

Mark looked up toward the house and there was his father setting on the buggy waiting for him to come up so they could go to town. When they arrived at the bank Will signed some papers to allow Mark to take out a loan from the bank to buy Willie from his father. Mark agreed to pay the loan off in three annual payments. When they walked out of the bank Mark asked his father if he could take the buggy down to Big Sean Davis's cabin?

His father said, "Yes, and if he's home why don't you bring him on up to the restaurant and we'll have something to eat and drink."

Mark said, "Okay," and took off to the little cabin on the outer edge of town.

When he got to Big Sean's cabin it was nested alone the side of a little creek where you could see skins hanging on lines from the little log cabin to the near by trees. Mark assumed they were from the last hunting trip he was on. As he pulled up to the little cabin Big Sean spotted him and came walking out to meet him.

"I'm not use to someone coming to visit me in a fancy rig like this," roared Big Sean as he stuck his large hand out to shake Mark's hand.

They were still shaking hands when Mark said, "First off, Sean, I want to apologize for our first meeting."

"Hold up there a minute, Mark," replied Big Sean, "you said you wanted to go on a hunting trip sometime."

"Well," he roared, "out there in the mountain country sometimes if you hesitate you won't be there tomorrow to apologize, so think no more about it, boy!"

Mark went on to tell Big Sean what had happened Sunday at the birthday party when Willie let it slip that he could read.

"You know, Mark," Big Sean said, "I thought that boy was poking a little fun at me so maybe that's why I pushed him a little too far."

Mark looked Big Sean straight in the eyes and said, "Sean, does that offer still stand on that hunting trip and when are you leaving?"

A little grin came across his large beared face as he replied, "It sure does, son. As soon as I get rid of the rest of these hides, which will be later on this week. We'll be ready to leave."

Mark's black eyes shined as he smiled and said, "I guess that means I'm going with you, doesn't it?"

"It does son if your old man can spare you for a few months."

" I'll be more then glad to go with you for six months, but there something you have to know and okay first."

"What's that?" inquired Big Sean.

Mark answered in a hesitant way as he looked up at Big Sean and said, "Sean, I got a problem." He went on to say, "I think you understand the reasoning of why my father had to take the whip to Willie and then sale him. Well I bought Willie from my father and asked for a six months leave in hopes that we both could go with you."

Big Sean sensed the worried look on Mark's face and said, "So what's the problem?"

Mark answered by saying, "I just I thought you might object."

Big Sean said with a roaring voice, "You know, Mark, an educated black boy might be just what we need up in them mountains at night when the camp fires burn down to scare them bears away. If they see them white eye balls with nobody they'll be climbing the trees trying to get away from us."

Mark laughed at Sean's remark and said, "Now, Sean, Willie will answer to you when you need his help, but I think you know my feelings on how he is to be treated."

"That I do, son," he replied, "so bring that boy with you and we'll plan on next Monday morning early to leave out."

Mark was about to step up to get on the buggy when he turned and said, "By the way, Sean, would you like to join my father and me up at the Pub for something to eat and drink?"

He said, "I sure could use a bit about now," as he grabbed the buggy with his big hand and pulled himself up to sit down on the seat. As they drove away, the buggy was leaning to one side due to the weight of his large body.

There dinner went well and while they were eating Mr. Howiton stop by the table and said hi to Will. He then turned to face Mark and asked if Willie was okay.

Mark replied, "Yes, he'll be okay, he just needs a few days for the wounds to heal."

Will spoke up and said, "Mark is Willie's new owner now and they are leaving with Sean Davis on a hunting trip out west." He then introduced Mr. Howiton to Big Sean.

Mr. Howiton was turning to leave as Mark stood up and walked with him to the door. At the door he asked him if it would be okay if he called on Sarah Saturday afternoon to take her to the dance Saturday night.

Before he went out the door Mr. Howiton turned, grinned at Mark and said, "You can call on her, but I can't tell you if she will accept or not." Then he went onto say, "If she does I'll expect you to have her home early and be at our house for Sunday dinner after church."

Mark laughed and said, "I believe I can meet all those requirements, sir," as Mr. Howiton walked away.

Big Sean was the first to get up to leave the table as he put his large hand out to shake Will's hand. He then said in a protective way, "I'll take good care of your boy, Mr. Cooper, you can be assured of that."

Mark's father looked up at the huge mountain man and replied, "I'm sure you will."

Big Sean then turned to Mark and said in a demanding way, "Are you tender foots going to be ready Monday morning bright and early."

Mark's black eyes snapped as he said, "Don't ever let it be said that a Cooper doesn't do what he says he's going to do!" In a more controlled tone, he went on to say, "But to ease your mind, we might just drop in Sunday night, late."

With a grin on his face Big Sean looked over at Will winked and walked away.

Mark's father said, "Son, I think it's time to get back to work and see how that boy's doing."

They both new there was a lot of work to be done before Mark and Willie could leave.

Chapter Nine
Mark and Sarah Set the Date

Willie's wounds held in a few days and the week went by fast. It was Saturday afternoon by the time Mark and Willie got all the work done on the farm and the packing for the trip.

Mark gave Willie his last minute orders and said, "I got to go get cleaned up and take Sarah to the dance, so make sure you are ready for Sunday night departure."

Willie grinned from ear to ear as he replied, "I sure will be Master Mark, sir! Mark had took a couple of steps toward the house when Willie said, "Mark, I will always be indebted to you for what you have done for me even if you was to set me free someday."

Mark hesitated, turn back to Willie and with a grin on his face said, "Willie, your desire for freedom my be tested in the next few months if them there bears start chasing us around the mountain sides a licking their lips." Willie was still in deep thought when Mark said to him "Willie before you do anything else hookup the horses to dad's buggy."

"Okay," replied Willie as he walked slowly away.

Mark was all dressed up when he asked his father if he could use his buggy.

His father replied with a grin by saying, "Well, I guess so, it would be kinda silly to unhook them now, wouldn't it?"

Mark grinned and as he walked out the door he heard his father say, "Now be carful."

"Does that mean with the horses and buggy or Sarah?" Mark asked.

His father said with a grin, "You know what I mean."

Mark was part way to the buggy when he turned and said, "Thanks, Dad."

When Mark pulled up in front of the house to pick Sarah up he thought to himself how lucky he was to be 21, a slave owner riding in a fancy buggy and taking the best looking girl in the county to a dance.

When Mark knock on the door it was answered by Mrs. Howiton as she invited him in and said, "Sarah will be right down."

They talked for a short time and then as Mark looked up toward the open stairway he saw the prettiest girl he had ever seen slowly walking down the steps.

His hart began to beat faster then normal as she walked over to him and asked, "Do I look okay?"

He was so nervous he didn't know what to say as his black shiny eyes looked into her deep blue eyes, he uttered the words, "Does heaven have stars? If it does," he said, "I'm looking at the brightest star in the universe."

Sarah smiled as she looked deep into his eyes adding to the anxiety he was going through causing his body temperature to rise above the safe rang. She then said, "I'll take that as a complement," as she put her hand out for him to take.

They then told her mother goodbye and walked out to the buggy. Before they climbed up into the buggy Sarah said, "Mark, you are just full of surprises, aren't you?"

He said, "What do you mean by that?"

She looked at him with a mischievous smile and said, "Not only do I get to ride in the fanciest buggy in the county, I get to ride with a the most handsome slave owner, too."

Mark replied, "That might be debatable by other people."

"But not by me," Sarah said as Mark held her hand to help her up into the buggy.

When they drove away Sarah was facing Mark and saying, "Remember I told you that you would do the right thing when the time came for you to make the decision about you and Willie." When the buggy left the house Sarah scooted over close to Mark and laid her head on his broad shoulders as they disappeared from view.

The sun was just above the horizon in the west when they arrived at the dance. When they walked through the door they both were invaded by people wanting to know what happened at the farm and of course very pleased to see the attraction that had developed between Mark and Sarah. Several young men including Joe Conklin came by that night to take their turn to dance with Sarah.

While taking his turn to dance with Sarah, Joe Conklin said, "You know, Sarah, the days and night can get long waiting for Mark to return home from the west."

She pushed him back as she said, "Not as long as they will be for you if you have any ideas of trying to court me while he's gone."

Joe grinned and said, "Sarah, that Mark is one lucky guy."

It was getting late in the evening when Mark said, "Sarah, would you walk with me outside?"

Both their body temperature had risen to a higher level do to the exercise from dancing. Then she turn her head to toss her long blond hair over her shoulder exposing her desire for him through her deep blue eyes. Mark sensed her desire for him as he took her hand to walk her out side.

She stepped closer to him while still looking up into his sparkling black eyes and said, "If I can wait that long?"

They walked out the door and down to the corner of the building. There they turned and walked out of sight of the people passing by. Mark turned to talk to her as she reached up and put her arms around his neck. He leaned over as he put his arms around her soft tender body and pulled her close to him.

Then just as there lips began to touch she said, "I wasn't joking honey!"

Mark then pulled her so tight to his body that his imagination gave way to the realization that their desire for each other was burning wildly out of control. He began to push her ever so gently away from him as her soft tender warm body resisted causing the temptation to be to great for him to over come.

He let her large well-developed breasts sink deep into his rigid muscular body as he pulled his lips away from hers and said, "We have to stop now, honey!"

She squeezed him even tighter as she smiled and said, "Now remember what you have to come home to." She gradually loosened her grip on him as they both stepped back.

Mark then looked deep into her magnetic blue eyes and said, "Sarah, will you marry me?"

She put her arms around his waist again as she looked up and said, "Yes, yes, yes!"

Mark put his arms around her and cuddled her close to his body. Then just before their lips met again Mark said, "Should I take that as a definite yes?"

When they came up for air this time Sarah replied to Mark by saying, "Is there any doubt now?"

Mark looked down into her eyes and said, "None whatsoever!"

Nature had done took over as their bodies penetrated each other, causing the desire to turn into a demanding call of the wild to fulfill the moment.

Just as Mark found himself ready to give into the boiling passion Sarah said in a very weak voice with a tear in her eye, "Oh, Mark, can we wait?"

Mark pushed her away and said, "Not only can we wait, we must wait."

For the first time Mark saw a sad look in Sarah eyes as she asked, "How long to we have to wait?"

He freed one arm from her body and wiped the tear from her eye and replied by saying, "Does six months sound too long for you to wait, honey?"

"Yes," she said, "but I would wait forever if had to."

"It may seem like forever, but it won't be," replied Mark as he took her by the hand and started walking back to the dance hall. While they were walking back they both came up with a date to be married.

Mark then said, "We should tell your mother and father tomorrow at the dinner the date we have selected." They both agreed as they walked inside the dance hall. They said their goodbyes to everyone and then left to take Sarah home.

On the way to her house Sarah said, "When you come over for dinner tomorrow why don't you bring your mom and dad over, too, then we can tell both families at the same time."

"That's a good idea, Sarah, but how would we get them there without telling them ahead of time?"

"Mom and dad are expecting you so I'll just tell them I would like for them to come, too. After all, you are going to be gone for six months."

"Yes, they would probably like that and not be surprised either." Mark reached over and pulled Sarah over close to him just before they came up to her house and said, "Now you know why I have to marry you, don't you?"

She ran her fingers through his black, wavy hair, smiled and said, "Why?"

He hesitated as to enjoy the moment of her fingers moving through his hair, then said, "Not only are you very, very, beautiful, you are smart, too."

She asked Mark to come in the house so her mother could ask him to have his mother and father over for Sunday dinner, too. Then Sarah asked her mother if it would be okay as they wouldn't be seeing him for six months.

She said, "Of course, by all means have them come."

Mark thanked Mrs. Howiton and gave Sarah a quick kiss on the lips as he walked out the door to go home.

The sun was rising with a brilliant red glow above the horizon in the east when that ever faithful rooster came out of the hen house and preformed his famous cock-a-doodle-doo. Mark got up and as he was dressing he thought to himself, *I'm sure going to miss this regularity and security when we're out there in the mountains where survival is the number one issue as you plan your day*. As they all set down for breakfast Mark told his mother and father that they had been invited to come to dinner at the Howiton family. They both excepted and his mother said, "Now you are sure they invited us?"

"Yes, Mom, and they both want you and Dad to come," replied Mark.

The breakfast was about over when Mark's father said, "Willie came over last night and read me some from the book you taught him to read from."

"Oh, how did he do?"

"He can read as good as you or I can."

"Yes, I know and I only thought him a little of the basic that I was learning at the time, the rest he taught himself."

His father shook his head and said, "It's amazing, isn't it?"

"Yes, Dad, it is," he replied. "Oh, by the way, thanks for allowing Willie a little bit of mercy at the end of your whip."

"I just wish it could have been more," said his father with a sad look on his face as he got up and left the room.

After church they all arrived at the Howirton family for dinner. They were all seated at the table when Mr. Howirton gave the blessing. Then as they rased their heads to begin to eat, Mark and Sarah stood up. Sarah then said, "Before we begin are meal Mark has something to say."

Mark put his arms around Sarah shoulders and said, "I have asked Sarah to marry me and she has excepted."

There was complete silence for a few seconds that seemed like a year as they all looked at each other in dismay. They knew that it might take place some day but not this soon.

Mr. Howirton was the first to break the silence as he said, "Well, this calls for a celebration. Something like this doesn't happen every day in this house. Wait for me to get the wine before we eat and we'll have a toast to the occasion."

Mark said, "Your daughter is one step ahead of you, sir," as he reached under the chair and held up a bottle of her father's favorite wine.

Sarah had put it under the chair before they came in the room. After the toast was made and all the hugs and congratulations done they all sat down to finish their dinner. By the time the meal was over they all knew the date and what each one would be wearing.

After the dinner was over Mark said, "Sarah, would you come walk with me?"

She smiled and said, "Yes," as she took his hand and walked out the door with him.

Mr. Howirton said, "You know, Will, if ever there was two people made for each other those two are it."

Will said, "There's one thing for sure; their desire for each other will be tested in the next six months, won't it?"

"That it will," replied Mr. Howirton as he took another sip of wine.

Mrs. Cooper and Mrs. Howirton by now were deep in the planning of the wedding.

Mark and Sarah were setting on a bench inside the gazebo that was facing the west when Mark said, "Just think, Sarah, I'll be somewhere beyond the horizon by this time next week." Mark seen the sadness in her face as he said, "I hate to leave you, Sarah honey, but I have this burning desire, it's like something is calling me to go west and can't explain why I have it."

Sarah put her finger on his lips as she said, "You don't have to explain to me, my sweet man, I have no intension of competing with that vision that's locked in that mysterious mind of yours, but I do want you to remember if that vision does become blurry just search your hart and you will always find me in there waiting for you in a place called home."

Mark stood up and took her hand as he said, "Sarah, honey, I have to leave because we have to get things done so we can leave out early in the morning." He put his arms around her and pulled her in close to his body as he raised one arm up and pushed her long blond hair back and over her shoulder. Then he said to her, "I am the luckiest man in the world." As he moved his lips ever so gently to meet hers their bodies gave way to the temptations of the moment as the spark of desire began again to burn out of control. They both sensed the demanding call of nature as they gently pushed away from each other at the same time and with hands together walked slowly back to the house. A little later they just simply said goodbye to each other as the view from their eyes reflected the image back to their harts that would have to last for the next serval months.

Mark was the first to move as he grabbed the handle on the seat of the wagon and pulled himself up to set down where his mother and father was waiting to leave. Sarah turned and walked slowly to the house where she turned and watched the Cooper's disappear to the west in the afternoon sun light.

Willie meet the Cooper's and took the team of horse so they cold go in the house.

Mark said to Willie, "I'll be out in a bit and we'll finish getting things ready to leave. After that we'll eat supper hear and then leave out and bunk down for the night at Big Sean's place so we can leave early in the morning."

After their supper was over and they said their goodbyes. Then they climbed up on their horses and rode off in the direction of town leading their pack horse behind them.

All of Mark's family and Willie's family had done left for their houses when Will Cooper looked over at his wife Ann and said, "Oh, to be young again." He then put his arms around her shoulder and started back to the house.

Chapter Ten
The Last Night Before Their Trip

The sun was starting to disappear below the horizon beyond the blue ridge as they arrived at Big Sean's house. Willie was given choirs to do to prepare for the trip out tomorrow.

Big Sean said to Mark, "I'm in the process of fixing something to eat. So come on in and you can look over the maps I've laid out showing the trails that we'll be taking through the blue ridge and Cumberland mountains."

While Big Sean was cooking Mark asked him, "How long it would take to get through the gap into Kentucky?"

"Well, we'll be hunting, trapping and trying to sell as we go so were probably looking at four to six weeks."

"Then how long will the supplies we have now last?" Mark asked.

Big Sean walked over to put another log in the open fire place where a back iron kettle hung above the fire. "We'll be wanting to put some miles behind us the first week," he said, "and hopefully are supplies will last long enough to get us into some good hunting area by then." He then walked over to the old plank table in the middle of the room where Mark was sitting and said, "Mark, I know you are growing into a yong man of high character with a vision of the future, but I got a feeling your desire for land is greater than your desire to hunt and trap."

He looked up at Big Sean with a grin on his face and a sparkle in his eyes and said, "It appears that your feeling serve you well, it must come from your close ties with nature." He then seen the concerned look on the big mans face as he said, "Sean, there's one thing you can be a shard of is that Willie and I will hold are end up. I can most of the time hit what I shoot at and Willie can probably clean them as fast as we can bring them in." He then leaned back in the old log chair he was sitting in as he said, "We're expecting to learn a lot from you, sir."

Big Sean looked down at Mark and said, "I'll teach you what I can, but there's one thing you should remember and that is when were out in that wilderness country nature can be your best friend or your worst enemy. So my advise to you son is to say alert, use common sense and only think about that pretty little lady you're leaving behind when you bed down for the night."

Mark said, "That's a tall order, Sean, but I'll sure take it under advisement."

Big Sean laughed and said to Mark, "Well, I guess it's time to get that boy in here so we can eat."

Mark looked at Big Sean as he stood up and said, "Sean, if you are uncomfortable with Willie coming into your house to eat he can take his meal outside."

Big Sean laughed with a loud roar and said, "No, Mark, when we eat from here on out that Willie boy eats with us wherever we go and I'm big enough to make it happen."

Mark laughed and said, "I'm sure you'll make a believer out of those who don't believe you."

Big Sean walked over to the door and yelled out in a loud roar, "Willie, get your hind end in her so we can eat!"

It was dark enough by then he could see the whites of Willie's eyes as he walked up the path to the little log cabin.

Big Sean turned to Mark and said, "I didn't think I was scared of anything until I saw them there white eyes coming at me in the dark with nobody!"

They both were laughing when Willie came through the door.

Big Sean rubbed Willie's kinky black hair and said, "Sit down, boy, you got some eating to do."

When Willie sat down he appeared to be a little scared. He then glanced over at Mark and saw Mark nodding his head in agreement with Sean.

Willie picked up his fork as he looked up with that big old smile and said, "Thank you, Master Sean, sir."

Big Sean laughed and said, "Hey, I like the sound of that, boy." He went on to say, "I think you and me are going to be getting along just fine. Now eat up," as he put his food on the table that was made out of log planks.

Mark said as he took his plate to put some food on it, "Don't take offense if we don't eat a lot as we just had supper about two hours ago before we left home."

Big Sean laughed and said, "No offense taken as long as you clean your plates up." He hesitated a moment, winked at Mark then he looked at Willie and said, "I'd hate to think that somebody didn't like my cooking."

Willie looked up and said, "Can I have more of them there potatoes, Master Sean, sir?"

They both were laughing as Willie took time from eating to say, "You sure is a good cook, sir."

After Willie had eat so much that he couldn't hardly move Mark said, "Willie, I think you need to work some of that food off so go get are bedding laid out for tonight."

Big Sean spoke up and said, "You can bring your bed rolls inside for tonight if you wish."

While Willie was out side Big Sean finished laying out the final details of the trip. Shortly after Willie came back with the bed rolls and they all bedded down for the night.

They awoke the next morning to the roar of Big Sean's voice saying, "We're burning daylight so let's roll!"

Mark looked over at Willie and said with a grin on his face, "See, Willie, I told you we didn't have to bring that old rooster with us, didn't I?"

Willie smiled and replied back, "You sure was right, Master Mark."

They got up to the smell of coffee brewing as Big Sean said, "It's best we eat light and get going, boys."

Mark and Big Sean was finishing their coffee when Mark told Willie to go harness the two horses in the barn. As he got up to leave he said, "Willie, take them out and hook them to the wagon and tie our pack horse on behind." By the time Mark and Big Sean walked out the door of the little log cabin Willie had all the horses and wagon ready to go. Mark said, "Willie, you done a good job, now you drive the team and wagon. Sean and I will be out fount."

"Okay," said Willie as he left to go get on the wagon.

Mark and Big Sean were climbing up on their mounts as Big Sean said, "That boy sure isn't scared of work, is he?"

"No," replied Mark. He then went on to say, "If he likes you he'll do anything for you." He looked over at Big Sean and said, "I think he likes you."

Big Sean said, "Well, what happens if he don't like you?"

"Then he'll do whatever he has to to survive," replied Mark in a stern voice as he looked Big Sean square in the eyes and said, "I would expect him to do just that."

Big Sean was looking into Mark's snappy black eyes as he realized for the first time that he commanded authority when he talked even to a man of my size and reputation.

They were by now going through town in front of the store where Mark had challenged Big Sean when he went to fair with Willie. The people on the side walk was waving their hands to them as they drove by. Mr. Lucas came out of the store where the people had gathered that day by the well and said, "Good luck, Mark." The three men were heading west out of town as he raised his arm to wave goodbye. He then said to the people that had gathered, "Now take a look at that. Isn't that a sight? The son of a wealthy planter, a roaring mountain man and a starry eyed slave boy all heading west out beyond the blue ridge." Then he shook his head, smiled and said, "The story is they're going through the Cumberland Gap into a place called Kentucky in search of free land."

Chapter Eleven
West to the Blue Ridge

The first night out after they were done eating, Mark looked at Willie, grinned and said, "We never had that arm wrestling competition on my birthday, did we, Willie?"

"No, sir," replied Willie.

Big Sean said, "What are you guys talking about?"

Mark then explained how down through the years on his birthday he always arm wrestled Willie and of course for several years he let him win. Then Mark said with a chuckle, "But last year I didn't let him win, he won on his own."

Big Sean walked over and grabbed Willie's arm and squeezed it, he then looked at Mark and said, "What have you had that boy doing to muscle him up like that?"

"Well," Mark replied, "maybe it's all that wood he cuts and splits so everyone can have fire for their cooking and heating of their cabins."

Big Sean said, "It looks to me like the Cooper family feeds their slaves well, too." He then turned to look at Willie and said, "Well, boy, if you're not going to take your master on. How about just an old mountain man?"

Willie looked at Mark as he nodded his head okay. Willie then said, "Okay, but you look to be much stronger than me, sir."

Big Sean said, "There's one way to find out, but you better put everything you got into it or I will tan your hide good!"

Mark set the table up so they could have a level spot to compete on. Mark set the rules and on the count of three dropped his hand and said, "Go!" Big Sean had been in numerous arm wrestling events in his travels down through the years and new that a quick snap of the wrist was a key to winning. He must of thought Willie being a big black slave boy would be a little slow. Well if so, he thought wrong. Willie's large black muscular arm snap his hand and wrist so quick that Big Sean found his arm moving slowly downward and helpless to pull it to a stop. He finally stop the downward motion of the big black arm just before his arm would have hit the table. He let out a loud roar and said, "Hang on, boy!" Willie's arm then started to move back to where it began. Before it got to top center, Willie put all the power that he could muster and pulled Big Sean' arm back down again. But he could not hold the mighty arm of the roaring mountain. Big Sean grinned, looked at Willie and said, "You got to have holding power boy if your going to beat the big man!" Willie by now had no feeling in his hand as Big Sean's powerful grip crushed down on his smaller hand like an iron vice on a piece of soft wood. Willie's eyes got larger as he helplessly watched his arm move up slowly through top center and began it's journey to the table below, slowly at first and then slammed hard against the table. When Big Sean released his mighty grip, Willie looked at his arm and hand to see if they were still attached. Big Sean reached over and rubbed Willie's kinky hair and said, "You are one hell of a man for an 18-year-old boy." He looked back as Mark shook his head and said, "He's the only man to ever put my arm that close to the table."

The forth day of their trip came to an end when they stopped close to a place called Patrick Springs.

Big Sean looked over at Mark and said, "We been hitting it pretty hard for four days now so I think it's time to hold up for a few days."

"You're the boss," replied Mark as he looked around and said, "Sean, this looks like it might be a good hunting area."

"That it is," replied Big Sean as he swung down off his horse.

Mark stepped down from his horse also, then they walked toward the wagon where Willie was looking west at the setting sun. Big Sean touched Mark on the shoulder and pointed toward Willie.

Then he said with a grin, "Willie my boy take a good long look at that view and see what real freedom is all about."

Willie was looking out at the panoramic view within in his vision when goose bumps began to rise on his large arms as he reached high above his head as if to grasp the moment.

He then said as he looked down at Mark and Big Sean, "Man should not lay claim to such beauty, but just enjoy as we pass through."

Big Sean said as he looked up at Willie, "I have to admit Willie, my boy, I think you're right. But I don't think the creator will mind much if we take some animals for food and some hides for protection for our bodies while we're here, do you?"

"No, sir, Master Sean," replied Willie.

Mark was looking at the view they were talking about when he turned and walked to the back of the wagon.

"Willie," he said, "when you get tired of looking at the view we got a lot of work to do to get camp set up."

"I don't think I'd ever get tired of looking out there so I guess I best just get started to work now," replied Willie.

He then got down from the wagon and walked back and started unloading the items needed to set up camp where they'd be staying a few days. Three separate shelters was set up for them to sleep in. The fourth shelter was set up around a makeshift table that was stored in the bottom of the wagon. It would only be set up if they stayed in a location more the one night. In between the shelters and the table they set up a tripod across the fire they had built to do their cooking. From the top of the tripod they hung either a iron skillet or an iron pot depending on what they were cooking.

The sun was going down below the blue ridge that was by now only a days ride by horse back away. The fire was roaring beneath the iron pot where Big Sean was cooking their first real meal since they left Buffalo Springs. Willie was coming back from the near by creek with water needed to prepare the meal and make the coffee. The seat from the wagon was setting on the ground facing the fire and the panoramic view of the famous blue ridge mountains that until now had only been a fragment of Mark's and Willie's imagination. Willie set the water on the table so Big Sean would have excess to it for cooking the meal. Mark was setting on the seat from the wagon looking out at the view that had by now toned down in brilliance. But it was still giving off a deep red glow as the sun began to loose its power.

Then he said, "Willie, come sit down for a bit and look at what we been dreaming about all our lives." They both set for several minutes in silences then Mark said, "Willie, is it something like you pictured it?"

"Yes, but something is strange about the sky," he said as he turned to look at Mark. "Do you remember," he asked, "how bright the glow was when the sun began to set above the blue ridge a little while ago?"

"Yes," replied Mark.

"Well," Willie said, "that's close to what I seen in my mind when I felt the first bit of the whip from master Will's hand." He stared into the fire for a moment then went on to say, "What I see now is that tone down peaceful look that I felt and seen in my mind's eye when the pain became less after each crack of your father's whip."

They both were setting in silence looking at the fire and the view to the west as the light of day began to give way to the creeping present of the dark of night. The roar of Big Sean's voice seem to awake them from a deep thought as they heard him say, "Unless you want to eat in the dark get those lanterns lit." Their meal was coming to an end as the lanterns offered a dull peaceful view of the campsite that would become their home for the night. After the tin dishes was washed and put away Big Sean said, "I don't know about you tender foots, but I got me a urge for something more then water and coffee to wash my meal down. There's a little place just down the trail a ways that can accommodate that urge."

Willie looked at Mark as if to ask if it was okay.

Mark got up and said, "Why not."

They all climbed upon their horses and rode off into the dark of night. The trail shortly offered a view below of several lights in the night and as they got closer they could make out the images of maybe seven or eight small log cabins clustered around a larger building. Then as they followed the trail on in they found themselves in fount of the larger building where three or four horses were tied up to a hitching rail. By then they could hear the sounds of laughter inside as Big Sean swung off of his horse and tied him to the rail.

He stepped up a couple of steps onto a porch where a few chairs were setting empty as he turned to Mark and Willie and said, "Well, come on in, let's see what that laughing is all about." He then pushed an old wooden door that didn't hang well open and roared out in a loud voice, "What are you little fellows doing making all that noise so a hunting man can't sleep."

There was one man behind the bar and four men in front that appeared to be hunters also. There were three or four tables in the room and one had a few men sitting around it. They all turned to look at the door where Big Sean was standing as the one behind the bar said, "Well, I'll be damned if it isn't the big man himself."

They all started toward him to shake his hand as one man stood up and said, "What brings you to this part of the country so early in the season."

Big Sean was stepping forward with his large hand out as he said to them, "I'll explain later, right now I got me powerful thrust to Quench." He looked a the bartender and asked, "Do you think a man can get something here to take care of that?"

The man behind the bar raised a bottle up in the air and swung it around. Then he asked with a big grin, "Do you think this well do the trick, big boy?"

His words were no more then out when a silence fell upon the room as Willie walked through the door followed by Mark.

Big Sean stepped on up to the bar then he reached out and took the bottle from the bartenders hand as he said, "This will do for starters."

"Now," he said in a roaring voiced "we'll be needing four glasses!" He then turn to Willie and Mark and rased his large arm up in motion for them to come on up to the bar. His voice rose to a loud roar with the words, "I'm buying, but I'm not a delivery boy!"

He began to fill the glasses when Charley Bob the bartender said, "Now you know, Sean, I can't serve that black boy a drink."

"I know," replied Big Sean as he handed one glass to Charley Bob then turned and handed one to Mark and one to Willie. He then said with a big grin, "Now you see you didn't serve him, I did!"

His hunting friends that had gathered around him were all laughing as they said, "He's got you there, Charley Bob."

Charley Bob was about to reply to the comment when Big Sean said, "Before this goes any further I'd like you to meet my new friends, Mark Harrison Cooper and his slave, Willie." He then went on to say, "Someone asked me when I entered this fine establishment what I was doing her so early in the season. Well," he said, "a few weeks ago I ran into Mark here, the son of a well-to-do planter. He says he wants to learn the art of hunting and trapping, but I think he's more interested in land down in Kentucky. In fact, I think in the back of his mind he may be thinking about that free land north of the Ohio River that someday will become a state called Illinois."

Mark spoke up and said with a grin, "It sounds to me like the big boy here has been doing a heap of thinking himself, doesn't it?" He then put his hand out to shake with the bartender and the other men standing at the bar.

They were all standing at the bar when they finished their drinks.

Mark looked at Willie and said, "Did you like that, Willie?"

Willie responded with a big grin by saying, "Yes, sir master Mark, sir."

Big Sean filled all their glasses again as he looked at Mark and asked, "Is it okay for the boy to have one more?"

Mark looked at Charley Bob as to show respect for his authority. He nodded his head in agreement as Mark replied, a thin smile below his coal black eyes, "Yes, one more!" He then said, "Willie, you take your drink over to that table and stay out of every one's way."

"Yes, sir," Willie said as he started to walk over to sit down. On the way to the table he bumped into one of the hunters and said, "excuse me, sir. I'm very sorry. Did I spill any on you?"

"No, boy," replied the hunter as he turned to his friend and said, "My god, did you see the arms on that boy?"

"Yes," said the other man, "but it's not noticeable under that large shirt he wears until he bends his arms."

Big Sean over heard the hunters conversation as he looked at Mark with a grin and said, "Don't you think it's about time for Willie to buy a round of drinks?"

Mark grinned and said, "Yes, I guess if the boy's going to drink he should at lease buy once in a while."

They both were grinning because they both new something that the bartender and the hunters didn't know.

By now the hunters were gathered around Mark and Big Sean wondering what they were grinning about as they looked over at Willie sitting by himself at the table.

Big Sean raised his arm up and said, "Willie boy over there, would like to buy a round for every one, but he's got a problem. He don't have any money." He then said, "Willie," in a loud roar, "would you arm wrestle any one in the house for a drink?"

"Yes, sir, Master Sean, sir."

"Okay, Willie. Now then, folks, if he wins, the challenger pays. If he loses his, Master Mark, pays."

He then looked at Mark and asked if that was okay.

Mark said, "That will be okay with me, but let me make it clear to the challenger if anyone will except. If Willie wins I will not tolerate abusive language or threats directed at him. If you can abide by those rules then let the contest begin."

One of the four hunters walked over to where Willie was sitting sipping very slowly on his second drink. He was being very careful not too drink to fast. The hunter walked around the table as he looked Willie over like a buyer at an auction. He was tall and slender built with long string brown hair and a bushy beard that make him look older then he really was.

He was making his second trip around the table when he said in a strong ruff voice, "Stand up boy!"

Willie said, "Yes, sir,"as he stood up and faced the would be challenger. The hunter looked back toward the bar and there walking in his direction was Mark, Big Sean, and the others were still standing at the bar talking.

Mark walked on over to Willie, gave him some money and said, "If you should lose, buy everyone a drink. Either way, win or lose after the drink Willie, we'll be going back to camp."

Willie replied, "Yes, sir, Master Mark, sir."

Mark turn back toward the bar and said in a loud voice, "If anyone else wants to look the boy over, feel free to come do so."

They all left the bar to walk over to the table as the tall bearded man said with a chuckle, "Bring the drinks with you, the boys about ready to buy!"

Mark's snappy black eyes caught the eyes of the bearded man as he said, "Well, sir, if you are going to be the one to challenge my boy, set in the chair across the table and I'll state the rules and give the start signal."

Everyone gathered around as the bearded man sat down across from Willie. Mark said, "Put your hands together and get a good grip." The bearded man looked Willie in the eyes and noticed how big they were when he heard Mark say, "Elbows together. If your elbow comes off the table you forfeit to the other person." He then asked, "Do you both agree?"

They both shook their heads yes.

He then said, "1-2-3-go!"

Willie was a split second quicker then the challenger on the snap, then the muscles of his big black arm began to bulge under his bulky shirt as the bearded man felt the power in his arm begin to fade. His arm was moving slowly downward as Big Sean said in a loud voice, "Come on, boy, I'm getting thirsty!" Willie looked up at Mark as if to ask for his permission. Mark nodded his head as Willie grinned and slammed the arm of the hunter down on the table with such force you could hear it across the room.

The bearded man jumped up from the chair he was sitting in and threw it across the room and said, "Damn you, boy!" Mark by now was standing in front of the bearded man with Willie behind him as his coal black eyes stair into the eyes of the bearded man.

He said very calm and very direct. "I assume, sir, you are a man of your word or you wouldn't be a friend of Big Sean Davis."

The other men that had gather around the bearded man said, "He's right, Dave."

Mark put out his hand and said, "If that's so, Dave, it would be an honor to have that drink with you."

Dave accepted Mark's handshake and said, "I just want to know one thing. Where in hell did you get that, boy?"

Mark laughed and sad, "Well, we didn't just get him we raised him."

Willie was still sitting at the table when they all walked over to the bar as Charley Bob the bartender filled all there classes.

Dave the bearded man looked over to where Willie was sitting and said, "Come on over here, boy, and have that drink with the men."

Willie stood up and looked at Mark. Mark nodded his head and motion for him to come on over.

Charley Bob the bartender was gladly filling Willie's glass when Dave walked over to Willie, ran his finger through his kinky hair and said, "You beat me fair and square, boy, so that makes you a man!"

Willie replied, "Thank you, Master Dave, sir!"

Dave said to Big Sean and Mark with a chuckle, "I think I know why you guys like that boy so much."

They all laughed as Big Sean said, "It does sound pretty good, doesn't it?"

They all held there glasses up and gave a toast to Willie, the most polite man in the house.

As Willie finished his drink little did he know that this would be only the first of many times that he would be the center of attraction or the center of conflict in the months and years to follow.

They all set their classes down as Mark said, "Okay, Willie, it's time to go."

Big Sean said, "Hold up a bit, boys. I'll lead the way back to camp." He then turned to the ones at the bar and said, "You see, boys, I gotta lead the way back because it scares the hell out of me to be back there in the dark and see those white eyes looking back at me with nobody."

They were all still laughing when Willie staggered a bit as he started for the door.

Back at the camp they were all bedded down for the night where Big Sean and Willie both were competing to see who could saw the most logs. Mark was laying there looking at the flames in the fire dance in the midnight air when for the first time since they left home he thought of how much he missed his Sarah. He remembered what Big Sean had said about only thinking of Sarah at night. A contended smile came across his face as he slowly fell off to sleep.

As the first ray of light from the rising sun began to show its presence, the by now familiar sound of a roaring mountain man clearing his throat and saying, "You gonna sleep all day!"

Mark and Willie both rased up and look at each other as Mark said, "Willie, how come you didn't bring that roaster like I told you, too?"

"I sure wished I had!" replied Willie.

Big Sean said with a grin, "That's enough of that cocky talk, we got some hunting to do today."

When the sun got brave enough to show it's face above the horizon the smell of bacon frying and the aroma of coffee brewing was in the air.

The next two days was spent going up and down hills and hollows as Big Sean tried to show Mark and Willie some of the arts to hunting and trapping different animals. It was getting on toward mid afternoon on the second day when they all stop to view a small creek running down from the mountain ahead of them. Big Sean rased his arm and pointed in a half circle motion as he said, "This is a good area for the animals to rondeau and wait their turn to sneak down to the creek for a drink." He went on to say, "The wind is blowing down stream so if we set tight for a bit and they don't pick up our sent we might see some activity shortly."

Willie asked, "Well, how comes they like this spot better than others along the creek?"

"That's a good question," replied Big Sean to Willie's inquiry. He then pointed to the surrounding area and said, "Willie, if you notice the area is offering good protection so they don't get trapped and can't get away while drinking."

Willie looked around to observe what Big Sean was explaining then said, "Master Sean, do you think there's any bears in the area?"

"Yes, Willie, there well could be." He then said, "Follow me and we'll ride down to that wooded area down stream from the water we see ahead of us." When they got to the wooded area they began to work their way up the creek until they seen the opening that Big Sean had pointed out. They then tied their horses up and went on by foot to get a better view of the rippling water flowing across the rounded rocks. Big Sean said, "Now if we'll be real quit and don't move we should see some movement shortly."

A few minutes had passed and a deer ventured out of the woods and slowly began the trip to the water below stopping ever few steps as if to be looking and lessening. When it finally made it to the water it began drinking and rasing it's head ever few seconds to look and lessen. Then all of a sudden it took off running at full speed across the open area to the where they were just at a short time earlier.

Mark had his gun up ready to shoot when Big Sean pushed the barrel down and put his finger to his lips and said, "Shoo." Then he pointed across the creek to the woods the deer came out of and there lumbering out of the trees was a big black bear.

When he got down to the water Mark rased his gun to shoot again as Willie looked up at him and said, "Master Mark, sir, are you sure you are close enough?"

Mark looked at Big Sean, Big Sean looked at Willie and said, "Well, if you get closer you could get a better shot." He then turned to Mark, winked and shook his head yes, while trying to keep from laughing out loud.

Mark pick up on what Big Sean wanted as he said, "Willie go on out in the opening and try to get a better shot."

Willie replied, "Okay," as he walked out in the opening then looked back as they both were motioning for him to go on farther out. He then stepped forward several steps and noticed that he could see the bear real good. Then all of a sudden the bear stop drinking, looked over toward Willie and moved his head in a circular motion and let out a loud roar. Willie rased his gun about the same time the bear lunged forward the shot rang out but he must of missed as the bear let out another roaring sound. He then turned toward the woods and said as he pass Mark and Big Sean, "I think I was too close!"

IN SEARCH OF FREE LAND

Mark and Big Sean both stepped out and shot at about the same time. One of the shots must of stunned the bear as he stopped, turned and rumbled off into the woods he came out of. Mark and Big Sean were both laughing as they walked back to where Willie was standing. Big Sean was laughing so hard that he had to put his gun down on the ground and hold his sides as he said, "Willie saved that bears life when he turned and ran because if that bear had seen those eyes it would have scared him to death!" He then walked over to Willie, grab him by the shoulder, pulled him close to his body. He rubbed his kinky black hair with his other hand and said, "Well, how did it feel to see that bear up close like that, Willie?"

Willie grinned and said, "Not as good as it did to see you two guys when I went by!"

Mark and Big Sean both were laughing at Willie's comment as Big Sean said, "Mark, you could have shot that deer, but don't you think it was worth the sacrifice to see Willie's first experience with a real live bear."

Willie was laughing by now as Mark looked over at him and said, "I wouldn't have missed it for nothing in the world."

They were all getting back on their horses when Big Sean said, "Let's go back downstream, check our traps and rebait them." He paused a moment and said as he looked at Mark, "Maybe you can shoot us some thing good for super with that fancy gun of yours while Willie and I run the traps."

Mark replied, "Okay," with a mile and said, "maybe I'll even get to shoot my gun this time."

Big Sean and Willie were just finishing up the traps and coming up the slippery bank when they seen Mark riding in with their meal for tonight hanging from his saddle horn.

They got back to camp a little early and was just finishing up their supper as the sun started to set in the west turning on the brilliant glow that magnified the panoramic view of the valley below. They all just sat for a short time not saying anything as each were deep in their own thoughts as time rotated the earth slowly to turn off the light for the night. Later on When Big Sean and Willie was sound a asleep and

Mark was laying down with his eyes closed and hands behind his head he seen Sarah running to the barn with her long blond hair blowing in the wind. Again a smile came up on his face as he gently fell off to sleep.

The next few days went by fast as they had to prepare the game they took so they could have food to eat and hides to sell. Then they would journeyed down the wester slope of the blue ridge mountains into the valley below. From there they would follow the wilderness trail to Kentucky. There would be small out post and villages as they travel southwest that would be in need of the hides for clothing that they could turn into cash. The settlers coming out of the northern states into Kentucky would be needing clothing and food as they moved into the new state. Big Sean, Mark and Willie of course would be trying to full fill some of those needs as they hunted, trapped and traveled the wilderness highway into the land of opportunity.

The morning of the six day of their trip the sun rose to shine down on the campsite as the aroma of coffee brewing filled the air. The wagon was all packed, the shelters down and the only thing left was the seat setting in front of the fire. As they sat around the fire Big Sean and Mark were looking at the maps as they sipped their coffee and plotted their next phase of the journey. Willie was finishing the chores, so as soon as they loaded the spring seat they would be moving out.

On their way to the top of the ridge they came across two more breathtaking views where they stop to rest their horses. The last one Mark broke Big Sean's rule and thought about Sarah for a few minutes as he looked out at the majestic view that was even more awesome then the one where they were camped at. "It later in time became known as Lover's Leap."

They were at the peak of the blue ridge that Mark and Willie had dreamed about all their lives. Big Sean seen they were enjoying the view as he said, "The horses need a rest and we do to after a day like that."

"What he was referring to was some where between the first scenic view and the second one they had to cut down four small trees and make two stretchers to pull behind two of the horses. Then they disassembled the wagon after it was unloaded and carried it on the stretcher through a part of the trail that was to narrow to safely pull the wagon. They then had to reassemble the wagon and make two more trips to pick up the items that was on the wagon and reload it."

They had only traveled about six to eight miles, but it was already getting late in the afternoon. They all came to an agreement that it was time to call it a day. They set a temporary camp for the night.

While they were eating, Big Sean said, "Willie, what did you think when we came upon that narrow path on the mountain side and couldn't go any further?"

"Well, Master Sean," Willie replied, "I thought we would have to leave the wagon 'cause I didn't know you could disassemble it like you guys did. I known one thing," he went on to say, "I was beginning to wonder about this freedom stuff before we got it across and loaded again."

Mark spoke up and said with a grin, "Willie, freedom sometimes comes at a high cost, doesn't it?"

"Yes, Master Mark, but it's worth every moment of it." He thought for a moment and said, "Mark, you have allow me a taste of freedom and I'll always be thankful for that." He then said, "Slave or free, I'll always be your servant."

Big Sean roared, "Well, boy, if you are still a slave, go get me some water from the barrel in the wagon so you can help me do the dishes!"

Willie jumped up and said, "Yes, sir, Master Sean, sir!"

There was about an hour of daylight left when Mark went to the wagon and got two books out. Big Sean was giving Willie a hard time as usual about one of the plates being dirty.

Mark walked over and gave one of the books to Willie and with a thin smile said, "When you guys get done playing with those dishes you can read this if you want to."

Mark and Willie were both in deep thought reading when Big Sean sat down next to Willie and leaned back against a tree. He then said in a loud voice, "Well, boy, how about reading to me you know I like a good story, too."

Willie marked the page and handed the book to Big Sean as he looked over and said, "I can read it later."

Big Sean looked out to the west to the endless miles of freedom and space before his eyes where he was master of his trade. Then he turned looked at Willie with a sad look and said, "Son, I can't read."

Willie looked at Big Sean with a tear in his eye as he said, "Master Sean, sir, it would be an honor to read you a story."

Big Sean reached over and rubbed Willie's kinky hair and said, "Thank you, boy," as he leaned his large bushy head against the tree.

Mark looked over his book and for the first time seen the bond that was building between the roaring mountain man and his starry eyed slave boy. He knew now that he would not be alone as they traveled if they came across any body that would not view slavery as he and Big Sean did. A contended look came across his face as he looked down and began to read again. They were still reading when Big Sean got up and lit the lanterns so they wouldn't quit. The moon was shining bright through the clear fresh air of the night as the lanterns gave off a dull peaceful view of the campsite where three men were about to become a part of history.

Chapter Twelve
West Beyond the Blue Ridge

The legendary stories of the three men would come to past in less the a week as they traveled the wilderness trail through a gap in the Cumberland mountains into Kentucky and beyond. There they would join with thousands of others with a burning desire to find land of their choosing. It was one of the first of many trails to the west that the settler's would use as they moved beyond their borders and through time curve out what came to be the most powerful nation on earth.

Again the sound of the roaring mountain man brought the camp to life as the sun rose above the Virginia mountains to shad light on the morning dew. The dampness was beginning to dry, as the wheels of the wagon started to turn carrying a black slave boy driving a team of horses closer to his dream of land and freedom.

On the downward journey of the western slope to the valley below they found them self's in the middle of a large meadows. The sun was at high noon and the horses need rest as Big Sean raised his hand to stop. After the noon break was over for the horses and men Big Sean said, "How would you guys like a good Pheasant or turkey super tonight." Willie looked at Mark as he nodded his head yes.

Willie then turned back to Big Sean rubbed his belly, rolled his big blue eyes around, smiled from ear to ear and replied, "That sounds good master Sean, sir!"

Big Sean looked at Mark grinned and said, "Willie, now we're going to need someone to flash them out and one guy on one side and one on the other side to shoot them as they fly up."

Willie grinned and said, "Well, why don't I flash them out but you better be fast 'cause if they take one look at me it'll spook them so bad they may die before they fly."

They were all laughing as Big Sean and Mark grab their guns and follow Willie as he was by now down all fours barking like a dog. Then he'd stop and act like he was pointing to a bird. After Willie quit acting silly Big Sean told him where to walk. Then shortly the sound of gun firing rang through the air as the order for Pheasant rotating slowly over an open fire was placed for their evening dinner. Back then known as supper.

After their supper was over and the sounds of discomfort from over eating had faded, Big Sean got up, put some water in a boul, set it in front of Willie, rubbed his kinky hair and said, "Good dogie."

Willie drank the water, barked twice and then on all fours walked over to Big Sean rased his leg as if to be wetting on his boot.

Mark's thin smile had turned into a real laugh as he said, "Do I have to put up with this nonsense the whole trip?"

Later on Mark and Big Sean were going over the details of where and how to market their product to the village store owners that they would be coming upon before long.

Willie had settled down by now and was coming back from attending to the horses for the night when he said, "Master Sean, the water is running low."

"I know," replied Big Sean. "There's a stream a few miles down the trail," he said as he walked over and got the book out that Willie was reading from the night before. This would be the first of many trips Big Sean would make to the wagon after super so Willie could read to him.

They woke the next morning and began their trip south by west. Then as they traveled the next twenty five or thirty miles Willie began to notice he was able to see the valleys to the east and the valleys to the west almost all the time. They stop for lunch at a point that allow them to see the view of both valleys at the same time. Mark and Willie were both gazing at the vast view that appeared to place them on top of the world. They both were looking to the east where they had came from and then to the south west to where they were going not speaking a word.

They both were shaking their heads in disbelief when Willie said, "The greatest writers on earth could not capture with words the emotions that flow through the body while casting your eyes upon such a view."

"Very well put," Willie replied Mark to Willie's unconscious statement.

Big Sean step between the two boys that had taken a large step across an invisible line that separates a man from a boy. He then grab their shoulders as he said, "Men, was it worth the pain and hardship coming up the east slop?"

Mark's thin smile appeared as he slowly shook his head still in disbelief. He then looked at Willie and back to Big Sean as he said, "Somehow, Sean, I think you know the answer to that question already."

Big Sean laughed as he shook his large head in admiration and said, "Even mountain men have to work, so let's get started, men."

The sun was starting set in the west when they stopped and set up camp for the night. Big Sean said, "Take a good look tonight, boys, for in the morning we'll be heading down the western slope of the mountain, leaving the blue ridge between us and home." Then as he looked out at the view before his eyes he said, "Within two days we'll be going down into a village where we'll be able to sell some of our goods to the people coming down the Shenandoah Valley from the north."

"How long will it take to get to Kentucky from there?" asked Mark.

"About seven or eight days," replied Big Sean as he walked over and got the book to hand to Willie.

Two days later it was getting late in the afternoon as they spotted a small village below that looked to be busy with activity. A little while later they came rolling into the edge of a small town as they passed some covered wagons that was stopped for the night. A couple of the men in the party raised their hands to wave as they asked, "Where you folks from and where you heading?"

Big Sean roared back by saying, "We're from Virginia on the east side of the Blue Ridge and we're heading for Kentucky."

One of the men that waved said, "We're from Pennsylvania and heading for Kentucky, too."

Big Sean said, "Well, good luck to you and maybe we'll see you along the way."

As they went by the wagons, Big Sean said, "We could set up camp here tonight, but I bet you boys wouldn't mind sleeping in a real bed tonight, would you?"

They both agreed it was a good idea.

Big Sean said, "We'll check in at the inn first. If they got a room and then maybe we can talk to some of the store owners and turn some of the hides into cash and food." He looked at Mark and Willie with a grin on his face and said, "Maybe we can even have a sit-down dinner tonight."

They pulled up to the front of the Inn and tied the horses to the hitching rail then walked inside. When they pushed the door open a bell ring, then another door open behind a desk across the room as a small well dressed man walked out.

When he seen Big Sean his eyes lit up and his facial expression changed from a serious look to a big grin as he said, "We were just condemning the devil and look who walks in."

Big Sean roared back by saying, "So you were back there praying I wouldn't come back to town, was you?"

"No, we were paying when you did come back to town that you wouldn't tear it up too bad," said the little man with a chuckle as he put his hand out to shake Big Sean's hand.

Big Sean reached out and shook his small hand and then grabbed him under the arms and tossed him up in the air like a father would their child. When he caught him on the way down he grabbed him by his shoulders and gave him a big bear hug. He then laughed and said, "Damn, I sure missed you, Johnny boy!"

"No," Johnny replied, "you just missed my cooking. Then he laughed and said okay big boy what are you up to now!"

Big Sean introduced Mark and Willie then he explained what they were doing.

Johnny said, "Have Willie put the horses in the stable for the night and give some feed to them." Then he gave some names of some of the merchants to contact for the hides to Mark and Big Sean. Before he turned to walk back through the door he came out of he said, "Will you be staying the night and having dinner with me?"

"If you'll have us," replied Big Sean.

"Of course you can stay," he said, "but I only have one room left so you'll all have to share it some how." Then as he started through the door he turned and said with a grin, "I'll be expecting you at my table for dinner in an hour and a half and don't be late."

Willie was starting for the door to take care of the horses when Big Sean said, "When you get done with the horses come across the street to the tavern and wait for us outside until we get there."

Mark looked at Willie and nodded okay as Willie went out the door to go to the stables. Mark and Big Sean contacted the merchants and made arrangements for the next morning to display their merchandise and try to come to an agreement on a price.

As they came out of the last place of business they were walking up the street to the tavern that they were to meet Willie at when Big Sean looked at Mark and said, "I don't know about you, but I got me a powerful thirst. How about you?"

Mark replied with a grin, "I'm so thirsty I could drain the Mississippi in one sip." He then looked at Big Sean and said, "Oh my god, I've been in your presence so long I'm starting to sound like you!"

Big Sean slapped Mark on the back and with a loud laugh said, "You know I have noticed an improvement in you lately."

They both were still laughing when they reach the bench in front of the tavern, but Willie wasn't there. Then Mark spotted Willie over at the stable and motion for him to come over. When he got over to where they were standing Mark asked him if he had the horses bedded down for the night.

Willie replied, "Yes, sir, Master Mark, they're bedded for the night."

Mark could see something was bothering Willie as he said, "Well, how come you didn't meet us over here like you was told to do."

Willie replied, "I did, Master Mark." He hesitated a moment and then said, "When I sat down on the bench to wait for you, some man came by and said to get off the street and stay over at the stable where I belonged. I tried to tell him that my master told me to wait here. Then he said, 'I don't care what your master said. I told you to get off the street and I mean now unless you want a good whipping.' So I went back over to the stable and waited for you like he told me to."

Mark then asked Willie if he could point the man out if he saw him.

Willie replied, "Yes, and went on to say he was about your size with long black hair that stuck out under his coonskin cap and had a large scar on his right cheek."

"Is that it?" asked Mark.

Willie shook his shoulders and said, "Well, sir, he had a demanding voice and a short temper."

"Did you see where he went when he left?" Mark asked.

Willie replied, "Yes, sir, he went in the tavern and hasn't come out yet."

Big Sean broke into the conversation and said, "I think I know the man he's talking about. He's called Scare Face Bob. I don't know what his full name is. But I think he's a hunter from Kentucky and hires himself out as a guide to some of the people coming down the Shenendoah Valley."

Big Sean looked into Mark's snappy black eyes and seen in them the determination not let this come to rest until it was settled.

He then said, "He's a loud man and has a tendency to intimidate most men. But if I were a betting man I'd bet his bark is worse than his bite."

Mark looked at Big Sean with that thin smile and said, "Well, we're about to find out how good a gambler, you are." He then pushed the door open and said, "Come on in, Willie."

When he walked through the door he motion for Willie to come and stand by his side. It was a small place with a bar the full length of the building with some tables scattered around. There was people at the bar and some sitting at the tables. They were all talking in loud voices and didn't notice Mark, Big Sean and Willie standing at the door.

Mark in a loud voice that rang out above the chatter in the room said, "I'm looking for a man named Scare Face Bob."

The room came to a complete silence as they were all looking at the three standing in the door and one was black. The room remained in silence for a moment.

Then a tall man wearing a coon skin cap stepped away from the bar in the direction of the door and said, "Just who in the hell wants to know?"

His scare was fully visible as Mark said, "Mark Cooper from Virginia, if you're the man that sent my slave to the stables, causing him to disobey a direct order from me."

"That would be me," said Scare Face Bob. "Now just what in hell do you think you're going to do about it?"

"It's not what I'm going to do about it, sir, it's what your going to do about it," replied Mark to his question.

Then as they stepped closer to each other, Big Sean stepped away from the doorway where Scare Face Bob saw him in the light and realized who he was.

He stopped his advance toward Mark and said, "Is that wild mountain man with you?"

"That he is," replied Mark.

Scare Face had seen Big Sean in a fight down in Kentucky a few years back where he had beat two men within inches of their lives and it took three or four men to pull him off the third one.

Mark stepped in font of Scare Face and said, "This problem is between us, not the mountain man."

Big Sean stepped on up closer to the two men and said, "Boys, I think I got a solution to your problem. My friend, Mark, here is expecting an apology for showing disrespect for his authority. Now, Scare Face, you don't really want to end up on your knees being forced apologize to a Virginia planter in front of all your friends, do you?"

"Just what makes you think it's going to end up like that," replied Scare Face Bob.

"Because I've seen you both in action and I can assure you that you are no match for this man," said Big Sean. Then he held his large arm up and said, "Even if you did win you still got this to contend with!"

The people that had gathered around moved back as his loud voice rang out through the small room.

Big Sean said in a more controlled voice, "I've seen you slam many a man's arm on the table with that big arm of yours in arm wrestling contests." Big Sean grinned and said well, "Willie boy here claims to the best one in Virginia." He then looked at the crowd and said, "Now, folks, wouldn't it be something to see a scared face mountain man and a starry-eyed slave boy go at it right hear in front of your eyes?"

They all yelled out, "Yell!" They clapped their hands and stomped their feet to a rhythmic beat trying to coach them on as some men cleared a table.

Big Sean held his arm up again and said, "Now wait a minute here, we got to have some condition before we begin." He then look over to Mark as he said, "Now if Scare Face wins, will you accept that as an apology, Mr. Cooper?"

Mark nodded his head yes.

Big Sean looked at Scare Face Bob and said, "If you lose, of course, Mr. Cooper will expect drinks for the house to be in order." He then grab Willie and Scare Face Bob by the arms and said, "If this agreeable to both of you gentlemen, shake hands and let's get this thing started."

They all started for the table, shouting, "Go, Scare Face, go!"

Some of the people that didn't like him or had went over and felt Willie's large black arm under his homemade oversized shirt were by now shouting, "Go, Willie boy, go!"

At the table, Mark set the rules and said, as he looked Scare Face Bob in the eyes, "If you should lose, sir, I will not allow undo barbaric language to be directed at my slave! Do you understand, sir?"

He replied, "Yes."

Then Mark gave the count to go.

A short time later, Willie was again the center of attraction in the middle of the white man's world as the clang of glasses toasted drinks in his honor.

Later they left the tavern and headed across the street to have dinner with Johnny. The dinner went well except a few comments from some people walking by their table about a black man eating in a white mans restaurant. By then some people had heard of the incident at the tavern across the street. After viewing the three men at the table with Johnny they didn't dare pursue their feelings except tipping of their hats or caps as they walked by.

After a good nights sleep they eat their fair well breakfast with Johnny. Then they conducted their business with the merchants and started off in a southwest direction with money in their pockets and some stable food in their wagon.

Chapter Thirteen
On the Wilderness Trail

They were now on the main trail that through time had become known as the wilderness road. It would intersect in a few days with the famed Daniel Boone trail. The next two days went fast so it was still mid afternoon on the second day when they came into the town of Bristol on the Tennessee border. As they went through town they noticed many more black people traveling with their white owners and some free blacks traveling on their own. They decided to go on through the village as they still had some daylight left.

When they left town Big Sean said, "By this time tomorrow we should be in Weber City on the old Daniel Boone trail."

The next day in the mid afternoon they came into the little village when Big Sean held his arm up to stop. He looked at Mark and Willie and said, "Boys, you are now on the Daniel Boone trail."

Mark looked at Big Sean with a contended look and said, "That means we're only about two days from Kentucky, doesn't it?"

"You're right," replied Big Sean. He then said, "It also means we can spend the night here," as he looked at Willie, laughing, and asked, "How's the arm feel today, boy?"

"Just fine," Willie said with a big grin on his black, rounded cheeks.

Mark grinned and said, "It sounds to me like you guys are up to no good again."

IN SEARCH OF FREE LAND

Big Sean said, "Let's stop and set our camp here where we can watch the people from the north and the people from the south mingle as they pass by on their way to Kentucky." He then added with a roaring chuckle, "Who knows maybe we can round up some competition for Willie boy here!"

Mark nodded his head okay and then said, "While you guys are conniving, I'm going to ride up town for bit."

He really wanted to talk to some one that might know about the land in Kentucky. He found out that a lot of the land in Kentucky up through the valley going north was getting pretty well populated.

Then one gentleman said, "There's still a lot of land straight west of the gap, but you got a lot of rough traveling to get there."

A short time later Mark arrived back at the wagon where Big Sean and Willie had the camp set up and a crowd had gathered. As he got closer he saw Willie and another black man setting across the table from each other with their arms together as he heard Big Sean count one two three go! The other black mans name was Moose and because of his size most people were putting their money on him. Bitting on arm wrestling back then was a high risk active as a few people found out that day when they walked by and placed their money in Big Sean's large hand.

Willie became pretty popular with the other blacks in the campsite in the next few hours. Even Moose finally came to Willie and shook his hand. Big Sean had ran into some of his old hunting buddies and were heading up to the tavern to toast the occasion. Mark had meet a man name Morgan who was heading for Kentucky with his family. After they talked they both agreed the best land would be west of the Gap even tho it may take a few more days to get there.

Willie and his new friends were laughing as they were all trying to imitate their masters. When it came Willie's turn to imitate his, he strutted out in front of all the others and looked then in the eyes as he tried to produce a thin smile on his big rounded face.

He then said, "I shall not allow any undo barbaric language to be directed towards my slave! Do I make myself clear, sir?"

They all laughed as Willie just didn't look the part of a sophisticated Virginia planter.

Mark was invited to the Morgan's campsite for super that night and some of the other slave owners invited Willie to a table they had set up for the slaves to eat at. William Morgan and Mark became good friends as they seem to have some things in common, such as the desire for land. When their super was over some of the people were walking back and forth up to the main part of the little village. Others were playing in the pasture where the horses were grazing. Some of the men were pitching horse shoes and some of the kids were playing hide and seek. Mr Morgan who by now Mark was calling Bill decided to walk up town to look around and Mark was in hopes he might run into Big Sean. Mark may have been worried about him as he had heard from some people that new him well claimed that when he drank to much he could become extremely violent when push to hard. They had walked in and out of a couple of stores and decided to cross a dirt path called a street to a tavern where they planned to stop and have a drink. They were almost across the street when they heard coming from the tavern a loud roar that sounded like a bull moose in an out house. Then they heard a thud like a horse kicking a side board off the barn as the rickety door sung out from the force of a mans body flying through the air. He had no more then hit the ground in front of them when the second man came flying out. The door flew open again as the third man was backing out and fell on top of the other two. About that time there appeared in the frame of the door way the huge body of the roaring mountain man. He rased his large arm and pointed his finger at the three men on the ground.

Then he said with a roar in his voice that almost shook the building, "If you call my friends slave that N word again you'll be spending the rest of your life in the happy hunting grounds."

Mark and Bill walked into the tavern where he introduced Mr. Morgan to Big Sean. Big Sean then introduced his hunting friends to Mark and Mr. Morgan

They then went to a table and sat down where Big Sean said, "The boys I had trouble with were slave traders. They have some slaves locked up down the street a ways in a wagon and their planning on taking them down to Tennessee and selling them on the market down there." He looked at Mark and said, "They must have heard about Willie and us and the arm wrestling incident." He then grinned as he said, "Then they made the mistake of calling me an N word lover."

Mark looked at Big Sean with that thin smile as he said, "Well, they may have been partly right Sean for I know one you do like."

Big Sean laughed and said, "You could be right. Maybe I just wanted a good fight."

Mark said, "I hope your need for a good fight was satisfied because I'd like to leave early in the morning and I don't really want to wet nurse a mountain man with a king size hangover, but if you feel the desire to have some more fun Willie and I can travel with the Morgan family to the Gap from here. Just make sure you catch up with us before we get there."

Mark and Bill Morgan got up and left the tavern as Big Sean said, "I'll see you before you get to the Gap."

The next morning Mark and Willie awoke to the hassle of a campsite preparing to leave as the sun began to peck above the blue ridge mountains to the east. The due from the clear midnight sky soaked their feet as they began to pack so they could leave out with the Morgan family. Sometime during the night Big Sean came by and picked up his riding horse and pack horse.

Willie by now had realized that he was nowhere around as he looked at Mark and asked, "Where's Big Sean?"

Mark replied by saying, "Willie, it's a long story, but he'll meet up with us at the gap in a few days." Willie's concerned look turned to a more relaxed expression as he began to finish up his chores.

The Morgan family were traveling with the Elie Cox's family so as they got ready to eat their breakfast they asked Mark and Willie to join them. When they sat down at the table Bill Morgan introduced Mark and Willie to Mr. Elie Cox and his family. Bill told Elie that him and Mark had been talking about maybe looking for land east of the gap instead of going north where it was getting harder to fine good land available.

Elie looked over at Mark and said with a grin, "Maybe there will be three families heading east after we get to the gap."

Mark replied, "Maybe we should wait until we gather more information about the area before we make a final decision. But it does sound like something we should consider."

The due was drying off from the heat of the early morning sun as the wagon's wheels began to roll leaving tracks in the grass where they had spent the night. Willie looked back over his shoulder at the tracks that was left in the grass.

Then he said, "You know, Master Mark, the tracks we leave behind today will soon disappear but I believe the image of those tracks in our minds shall endure for generations to come."

Mark looked over at Willie with a grin and said, "Willie, it sounds to me like were about to write some history. Now if that's true maybe we best be laying down some more tracks before we run out of time."

The next few days took them by several points of interest dating back into the seventeen hundreds. During that period of time the Indian trails were the only means of traveling into the wilderness of the new frontier now known as Kentucky. They were now traveling in an area where two of these old trails ran together for short while. One was The Great Worriers Path and the other known as the Wilderness Trail. As they followed this route now known as the Daniel Boone Trail they would be leaving the great Virginia Valley and passing through Moccasin Cap in Clinch Mountain. They would then inter into the interior of the Alleghenies. While following this road that was at one time just a path they could hear the old timers that had traveled it before talk about such things as the Devil's Race Path, The Natural Tunnel and of course the legendary tales of Daniel Boone. By the time the party had reached what is now Middlesboro, Kentucky, it was becoming hard to tell the difference between the truth and the myth.

Big Sean had keep his word and was at the east edge of a small settlement waiting for the party to arrive. When the party pulled up alone side of the three mountain men Big Sean raised his hand and said, "Hello, boys. What took you so long?"

He then said, "We got bored waiting for you folks so we done some hunting in are spare time and would like to offer you all some deer meat." He looked at Mark and Willie and said, "It's our way of saying welcome to the real frontier."

IN SEARCH OF FREE LAND

They all dismounted to rest for a few minutes before going on into the settlement, as they all turned back to the east and seen the dip in the mountain range called the Cumberland Gap.

Willie looked at the opening in the mountain and back to the west at the vast frontier that appeared before his eyes and said to Mark, "Oh, what a sight!" Mark was looking to left and then to the right as his cold black eyes seemed to be penetrating the wilderness wonderland like and eagle in search of free pray. At that moment in time as the party of men and women gazed upon their Garden of Eden, their minds was busses building the imaginary high way to success.

Mark brought the party back to earth by saying, "Ladies and gentlemen." He hesitated a moment as he looked to the west and said, "We have been invited into the home of the Almighty he asked that we take what we need, preserve what we don't need and pass our wisdom onto the next generation."

They all said, "Amen," including Big Sean and his mountain men friends.

The men and women had began their short trip to the small settlement below as Mark turn to take one more look back at the gap in the mountain. There he saw in his mind's eye the image of Sarah lying in bed, waving to him to go on and search for his dream. He then mounted his horse, looked back at the gap with a smile on his face and said, "Let's go, Apple Bee."

The party set up camp at the edge of the little settlement and spent the next few days stocking up supples that they might need on the trip west. Big Sean had never been west of the gap as he generally went up to the north but a friend of his new about the trails west. So they all agreed on a basic route that was laid out and would start their trip early the next morning. The settlement had become a busy place as it was one of the earliest routes across the mountains south of the Ohio river. Some of the families coming through the gap were in search of free land, the land before it became a state such as Illinois. Some were contented to settle in a new state such as Kentucky where the land was still available and much cheaper then the land back east.

The party Mark was with had decided to look for land straight west of the gap about one hundred miles where the farming might be better but still offer some good hunting grounds. Mark by now had his heart set on going on to Illinois after he heard some stories about the land between two rivers. One being the mighty Mississippi and the other now known as the Wabash. Between the two rivers lay the panoramic view of the endless miles of prairie where the grass was taller then your horse and could be seen for hundreds of miles. It appeared to look like a great ocean. There was stories of huge covered wagons called prairie ships that would transport settlers into the area. There were also stories of a large river called the Illinois that was said to be a hunters paradise where small rivers would dump the prairie water into the Illinois down the Mississippi to New Orleans. Mark's imagination was running way with him as he visualized farming the land between the rivers. There he would be able to sent his goods to New Orleans by boat down the river that seemed to be designed by a great architect just for that purpose. He was awoke from his trance as the sound of a bottle being slammed down on the bar where he was earlier having a toast to the new land.

As is he woke from his trance he heard the roar of the mighty mountain man as he said, "Come on, boys, who's man enough to take on the little slave boy here in an arm wrestling contest?"

Then another roar came from the crowd as a huge man said, "Well, big boy, how much you gonna pay me when I stick the boy's arm through the table top there."

"Well," roared Big Sean, "that's kinda up to the fine patriots of this fine establishment. Come on, boys, dig deep and let's see if the big man here can put the little slave boys hand through the table," he said as he nodded for Willie to remove his large oversized shirt from his body.

The men with money in their hands were, by now, observing both men carefully as they whispered to each other, "My God, look at the arms on that boy and he's got scar on his back, too."

Willie began to move in the direction of the rustic looking table, he then turn to look at Mark as if to ask for his okay. Mark nodded his head and Willie walked on over to the flimsy little table with a smile on his face. By then the crowd was about sixty forty for the huge man that looked like he had just came in from the mountains. His cold black stringy hair and beard cover his head, leaving a weather beaten face that housed two beady eye balls to identify him as a member of the human race. The cloths he was wearing looked to be made from the skins of the animals that he must of over powered with his long barrel gun that always appeared to be with in arms length of large body. Big Sean must new or heard of the man that was about to try and put Willie's arm through the flimsy looking little table, that was by now surrounded by people with money in their hands and ready to place their bets.

Before Big Sean started the countdown he said, "Okay, Wild Bill, let's see what you got?"

All was silent for a short time but didn't last long as the wild barbaric sounds of the big man began to filled the room. His curses were so violent and directed at Willie in such a roar that it caused Mark to get up from his chair and move closer to the table. A few more seconds past by before the sound of the flimsy little table shattering over came the roars of the mountain mans voice.

When the arm of Wild Bill went through the table his other arm was reaching for his long barrel gun as he said, "Your one dead black boy!" His arm was still searching for the long barrel gun as he looked up and seen the butt of it going at him just before the heavens opened up and showered stars all around him. As the stars faded away he saw the barrel end of the gun a few inches from his face.

The hammers were pulled back when heard the sound of a voice saying, "My slave will be expecting an apology sir or you can pick your head up on your way out."

When Wild Bill heard the demanding voice of Mark Harrison Cooper he realized his world could end shortly as he said, "Anything you say, sir!" Wild Bill got up and made his apology by saying, "You're the strongest damn black boy I've ever seen."

Big Sean looked at Mark and asked, "Is that good enough?"

A small thin smile appeared on Mark's face as he said, "Considering the sores, I'd say it's the best we can expect."

Mark turn to leave as he said to Willie, "You'll be going with me now."

Willie said, "Yes, sir, master Mark, sir," and followed him to the door.

At the door Mark turned and said Sean, "I'll be expecting you early in the morning."

The next morning found over half of the settlement preparing to leave in all directions even some going back east through the gap.

The party Mark and Willie was with would be traveling north for about fifteen to twenty miles through a break in the mountains now known as the Kentucky Ridge. Then they would be going south in what appeared to be a valley between two mountain ranges. After two days of traveling through what seamed to be endless ridges and valleys they came to the Cumberland river where they spent the third day out from the Gap hunting and fishing and enjoying the beauty of the wild west.

The forth night they stayed in a little settlement later call Williamsburg. The settlement was on the river east of a large Forrest that was said to be fifty miles wide and extended northeast almost to the Ohio river. Every one in the party agreed to stay over night and leave early the next day to travel through the majestic Forrest of large trees that lie west of them.

By noon the second day out they were leaving the Forrest and started seeing land that was suitable for farming east of the town of Monticello. The party agreed to hold up a few days and look the country side over to see if maybe this was where they wanted to plant their roots.

The afternoon went by fast as they were all busy setting up temporary quarters to stay a while. Mark, Willie and Big Sean had their shelter up just before the sun set in the west as the fire flaring high prepared the logs to cook the evening meal. Big Sean was preparing the meal, Willie was helping Eli Cox fix his wagon and Mark was visiting with Bill Morgan.

Shortly Big Sean said, "Let's eat, boys."

The sun was disappearing by now in the west beyond the reach of man leaving a bright red glow as Mark lit the candles and set them on the make sift table.

Willie was coming back from the wagon job and was walking toward the table when Big Sean said, "Wash your hands, boy!"

"Don't boy me, little fowler," replied Willie with big smile on his rounded face as he started to set down.

Big Sean reached out as if to grab him when he said, "You'll think, boy, if I get a hold of you."

Willie started running away when Mark looked up and said with a smile, "You guys sure know how to make the hardship of frontier living seem like fun."

After the meal was over Mark made his nightly trip to the wagon to get the books for him and Willie to read. After he had read for a while he looked up to rest his eyes from the glow of the candle light glare on his book as he seen and heard Big Sean trying to read to Willie. They had been practicing every night that they could and he was finally reading some.

A big grin was on his face as he looked up at Willie and said, "How am I doing, boy!"

Willie looked at Big Sean and said with a grin, "Not too bad for an old mountain man."

They both fall off to sleep shortly that night as Mark lay there looking up at the moon and stars shining down on the isolated land of the Kentucky frontier. Then suddenly he felt the presence of Sarah laying beside him as he moved his hand ever so slowly to touch her imaginary body. His face began to fill flash as he heard her voice say, "I need you, my love." The flush feeling left his body as he slowly raised his head to see if she was there. He laid back down with a disappointed look on his face and slowly fell off to sleep.

Chapter Fourteen
Back to Virginia

Mark awoke the next morning and knew he had to go back to his Sarah. After a husky breakfast he shoved his plate to the side and said to Willie and Big Sean, "I have something to tell you both."

He hesitated as he sipped his coffee and said, "I'll be going back tomorrow."

They both looked startled as Willie asked, "Why, Master Mark?"

"I can't explain it, I just know that I got to go back."

Big Sean grinned and said, "That love bug got you, didn't it, boy?"

Maybe Mark replied as he looked at Willie and back to Big Sean. With a concerned look on his face he said, "You know I can't have you two running together with the reputation that has followed you both in the last few weeks." He then said with a sad look, "Sean, I know by now you could never be happy without your mountains and Willie I know you want to continue on west. So I'll be talking today with Mr. Cox as I think he would like to go on west. If so, I may make a temporary loan of you to him if he would take you with him."

Big Sean spoke up and said, "Well, it's true I love my mountains, but you know I think I'll go with them to see how this plays out. Who knows, they may just need the help of an old mountain man like me."

Mark walked over to Big Sean and said, "That does ease my

concern about his safety, but I do expect your word that you will not hold any arm wrestling contest with Willie while I'm gone."

Big Sean put his large hand out to shake Mark's hand and said, "You can count on me, boss." He then said, "I take it your coming back then."

"Oh yes," replied Mark as he was shaking Big Sean's hand. You know he went on to say, a month out in the wilderness with a wild roaring mountain man and a big husky starry-eyed slave boy can change one's perception of reality."

Big Sean laughed and said, "It was fun, wasn't it!" He then left to do his morning choirs.

After Big Sean left Willie came over to Mark and said, "Thank you for letting me stay, also will you tell Mom and Dad a little bit about what we saw and tell them I love them."

Mark ran his fingers through Willie's kinky hair and said, "You know I will, Willie." Then Mark said, "Saddle up Apple Bee and bring him over to Mr. Cox's shelter. I think Mr. Cox, Mr. Morgan and I are all going to look at some possible land sites today."

By the end of the day the three men had came to an agreement on what they would do. The agreement they all came to was that they would pool their money three ways and Bill Morgan would stay and perches three forty acres section. Then Eli Cox would go on west after he helped Bill get settled in, which could take a few weeks. There he would perches three forty acres section. Eli agreed to the loan of Willie from Mark and Big Sean would stay on to help guide them through the rolling country of hills timber and rivers to some farm land they heard about near a settlement called Russellville. Mark would then maintain ownership of one forty acres a joining the Morgan eighty and Cox's eighty. Bill Morgan agreed to stay on his land even if he got the urge to move on until Mark returned with Sarah. Mark would leave the next day for home back in Virginia. Mark and Sarah were to be married in less the a year so in the mean time he would stay on with his father. The contract was put on paper, signed, witness and each man had a copy. The three men shock hands and agreed it was a good plan.

Mark turned to Willie and said, "Willie, you'll be taken the wagon and pack horse with you, when Mr. Cox leaves to go west. I'll be trying to travel as fast as I can so fix me up a pack to go with me on Apple Bee that will last three or four days. Most of the stops on the way back I can make in three or four days."

The sun was setting as they finished up their last meal together. The rest of the evening they spent looking up at the stars as the moon cast its spell upon this party of men and women that became a part of the Kentucky history. Shortly Mark fell off to sleep with a smile on his face while Big Sean was trying to read to Willie. The next morning Mark was long gone before they awoke.

Several days later Mark found himself in a small valley in the rolling countryside of Virginia. In less then an hour he was pounding on the door of the Howirton Family home. As he waited for some one to answer it seemed like an hour but was only a few minutes. Then Mr. Howirton answered the door and acted glad to see Mark as he stuck his hand out to shake Mark's hand.

He then put his arm around Mark's shoulder and said, "Sarah has been close to death, son, and had been asking for you up until about three days ago."

About that time Sarah's mother came into the room and seen Mark as she ran and put her arms around him and said, "God has answered our prayers."

Mark asked Mrs. Howirton how long Sarah had been sick.

She replied by saying, "About three weeks."

"About the time I left Kentucky," Mark said with a concerned look on his face. He then ask if he could see her.

She replied, "Of course, Mark," as she led him to her bedroom. Before they entered her room Mrs. Howirton said, "Mark, she came down with a bad cold and keep getting weaker each day. Then about three days ago she fell into a comma and hasn't responded since." When they reached her bed Mrs. Howirton said, "Sarah, honey, Mark's here."

She didn't respond so Mrs. Howirton said, "I'll leave you two alone."

After she left the room Mark took Sarah's hand in his hand and squeezed it gently as he leaned over her body and placed his lips on her lips. He then moved his lips back from her's and said, "Sarah, my darling, I'm so sorry I wasn't here when you needed me." Then he bowed his head and said a prayer that ended with the words, "For you have become the reason the purposes and the meaning to my life." The word life was still passing through his lips when he felt a small tiny hand squeeze ever so gently against his.

When he raised his head up and opened his eyes he found them looking into the deep blue eyes of Sarah and heard her say in a little whisper, "I love you."

Mark heard a knock on the bedroom door and then the doctor walked in. After he examined Sarah he shook his head in disbelief and asked her how she felt.

She displayed a little smile then turned her eyes to look at Mark and said, "Okay now."

The doctor turned to Mark and Mrs. Howirton and said, "I believe we should all leave the room now so she can rest." The doctor of course wanted to talk to the family alone. He told Mrs. Howirton the last time he was out that Sarah's fate was in Gods hands. He then turned to Mark and said, "I thought you were to be down in Kentucky for six months."

Mark grinned and said, "Well, Doc, you won't believe this, but about three weeks back down in Kentucky I laid down one night and was just looking up at the stars and the moon when I heard Sarah's voice plain and clear saying I need you, honey." Then he shrugged his shoulders and said, "So here I am."

Mrs. Howirton said, "It's a miracle, wouldn't you say, Doctor?"

The doctor put his hand on her shoulder and said, "Yes, it appears that way, but I don't think we should put the horse ahead of the cart just yet as she still has a long way to go to get well."

Mark said, "Doc, I haven't been over to the farm yet so do you think it would be okay if I went in to see her a few minutes before I leave."

The doctor looked at Mark and said with a little grin, "Well, it appears you're the miracle maker so I guess it'll be okay, but don't spend too much time until we find out a little more about her condition."

Mark entered the room and walked across to the bed, Sarah's eyes opened as she took her hand and patted gently a spot on the bed for him to sit. She then took her finger and put against his lip then slowly put it against her lip. Mark then moved his body slowly over her body and ever so gently placed his lips against hers. They both looked into each others eyes and knew they could never separate again for a long period of time. She was asleep still holding his hand as Mark gently removed his hand from hers and slowly left the room.

A short while later Mark was on the hill over looking the farm below that he knew so well. It was getting dark by now as he spotted the slave cabins that surrounded the house where he grew up as boy. Before he put Apple Bee in the stable he seen a light on at Willie's mom and dad's place so he rode down dismounted and knock on the wooden door to the cabin. Willie's mom answered the door.

When she saw Mark she through her arms around him and said, "It's so good to see you, Mark."

Mark said, "It's sure good to see the both of you," as he shook Willie's dad's hand.

Willie's mom then asked how Willie was doing.

Mark replied by saying, "Willie's okay and he wanted me to tell you all about Kentucky and the frontier. So I will be down to tell you all about it in a few days." He then sat down at an old wooden table that he remembered so well from the memories of his childhood days. They were all sitting at the table when Mark said "your son is no boy anymore. He has earned the respect of many white mem and has taken to the freedom of the west like a duck takes to water." Mark looked at both of Willie's parents and said, "He also wanted me to tell you both that he loves you and he would never forget his family." As he got up to leave he said, "Mamie, that's what he called her when he was a little boy. Then he put his arms around her and said with a serious look on his face, "Willie will probably never be able to come and be a slave again but I believe he admires the both of you for being so loyal to my father." As he started for the door he turned and said, "Willie is still my slave and I have loaned him out to a Mr. Eli Cox and they are going on to the south central part of Kentucky to purchase some land." He told them about Sarah and why he came back. As he opened the door to leave he said, "Oh, by the way, after Sarah and I are married we will be going to join up with Willie and Mr. Cox near the settlement of Russellville, Kentucky." When Mark closed the door he seen the two of them with arms around each other and tears of contentment gently sliding down the rounded cheeks of their face.

Mark rode over to the barn to put Apple Bee away for the night where he passed the door that he and Sarah would remember the rest of their lives. It was the time when he went to far and they both got a sever bite from an aggressive love bug.

When he entered the big house it was getting late so he stopped in at the kitchen to see if he could find some snacks. His mother was in the parlor reading and his father was in his office doing some late night work. The rest of the family was already asleep. Mrs. Cooper thought she heard a noise in the kitchen so she walked quietly over to the office and said, "Will, I think someone's in the kitchen." Will stood up reach over on the wall to grab a gun and moved slowly to the kitchen. When he stepped into the kitchen the gun was up on his shoulder and ready to fire. He then seen a image but couldn't make it out in the dime light.

As he moved his head slightly to the left he heard the sharp voice of Mark as he said, "Dad!"

He lowered the gun and said, "Son!"

Before they could say anything else Mrs. Cooper had her arms around her son saying, "Oh, how we missed you, Mark!"

Mrs. Cooper got some food and made a fresh pot of coffee as she new her son was tired and hungry. Both of his parents sat and lessened as Mark told them the stories about Willie and Big Sean and their adventures in the wilderness beyond the Blue Ridge. They new Sarah had been sick and had been over a few times to see her. When Mark got to the point where he was telling them why he came back so soon they both looked at each other as to say we know the feeling. Mark's mother said, "That was a miracle you having that vision. Don't you think, Will?"

Will looked at his wife, Martha, and said, "Honey, you know the mind of a young man in love can be a pretty powerful thing." He then reached over and took her hand in his.

Mark looked at both of his parents and for the first time realized how close their were as he could see the attraction of love flow between their eyes. Mark's mother took the dishes over to wash them as Mark and his father finished up the pie that she had made earlier in the day. They both pushed their plates to the side, lean back in their chairs and made some sound gestures that was meet to be a complement to the cook. Mrs. Cooper looked over at her two men and allow a small grin to appear on her face.

Will Cooper was the first to speak as he asked, "Well, son, what's your plan now?"

Mark thought for awhile and then said, "Well, Dad, I can't leave Sarah and my desires to go to Illinois is even greater then my desires was to go to Kentucky." He then looked at his father and said, "Dad, life is starting to get complicated."

His mother came by the table and asked him, "What was so fascinating about this Illinois he was talking about?"

Mark looked both his parents in the eyes and said, "Mom, Dad, can't you just see and image thousands of acres of land as level as the floors in our house filled with corn and wheat?"

"Yes," replied his father as he thought a moment and said, "I can also image how many slaves we'd have to have to farm that much land." Mark started to say something when his father interrupted him by saying, "And do you realize the number of field bosses and black whips you'd have to have to control that many slaves." He then asked with a grin, "And where would you market that massive amount of products?"

Mark by now realized he had gotten a little carried way with his story about Illinois to his conservative father.

He then displayed a grin and said, "I guess I've been out with a starry eyed slave boy and a roaring mountain man just a little to long, haven't I, Dad?"

His father laughed and said, "Well, son, maybe we should talk about Kentucky and this Illinois sometime in depth, but in smaller dimension."

Mark's laugh turned to his trade mark thin smile as he looked at his father and said, "In answer to your question about what my intentions are, the truth is I'm not sure." Mark's face took on a serious look as he said to his father, "Maybe I need to learn a lot more about the real business of farming and maybe even learn how to use that long black whip of yours."

A pleasant look came over his father face as he said, "Now that's the type of talk I like to hear."

Mark said with a grin, "Does that mean I got the job?"

His father replied by saying, "If you can keep tho's wondering feet in one place long enough to take on some roots."

Mark looked at his mother and back to his father and said, "Dad, it's been my experience in family farming that some roots grow deep and some grow outward but always stay attach to where they were planted."

Mark's mother spoke out and said, "I don't think we should doubt each others loyalty anymore as it's pretty plain to see it's well and healthy." She then walked over to a cabin in the kitchen and pulled a bottle and two glasses from the shelf and brought them over to the table. There she poured the wine into the two glasses handing one to her son Mark and the other to her husband Will. Now she said I think it's time for my two men to have a toast to their beloved land whether it be in Virginia, Kentucky, or a place called Illinois."

After the toast, Will said to his son, Mark, "When you get done with your choirs in the morning come up to the office as you got some catching up to do on some of our plans." He then started to walk out of the room with Mark's mother when he turned and said to Mark, "son work with me as long as you can, but when you have to leave I'll understand."

Mark said, "Thanks, Dad," as his mother and father walked out of the room.

Mark and his father worked together for a few weeks, some times in the office and some times in the fields. Each day they would set aside enough time for Mark to practice the art of handling the long black whip. As time slowly past by he became good enough at his new skill to draw his fathers attention. Sometimes in the evenings he would find time to make it over to see Sarah. Sarah, by now, was getting better by the day.

Then one Sunday the Howirton family arrived at church with Sarah and the rest of the family. Mark and Sarah of course were seen by everybody as they walked to their seats together. After the church services were over they invited serval families over to their house to pay respect for their loyalty during Sarah's illness.

Before the dinner was served Mr. and Mrs. Howirton thanked each of the families for their help and support during their trying times with Sarah. After dinner, Mark and Sarah asked to be excused and then left the house holding hands as they strolled into a near by pasture. Shortly, they found themselves looking deep into each others eyes as the volcanic eruption of emotion spilled out causing the violent movements of their bodies to cling together with one flowing desire. Once again the powerful will power of Mark prevailed as he looked even deeper into her magnetic blue eyes and said, "Honey, we must wait."

They then walked slowly to the house as they both realized that the call of nature my be more then they could endure over the next serval months. When they reached the end of the meadows and entered the back yard of her home they both turned and looked deep into each others eyes while keeping a distance between their bodies.

Mark was the first to speak as he said, "Sarah, honey, I think you know as well as I do that this flame of passion that roars inside of our bodies cannot be tamed by a mere stroll in the meadows anymore." He reach up to rub a tear from her eye as he said, "We have both been raised to wait for each other for that very special day that has already been set and I know it means so much to you and your family." He looked down at the ground for a moment and then rased his head, looked into her eyes and said, "So I'll be helping my father finish up the harvesting." Then he said with a sad look on his face, "I'll be going west to check on Willie and my land in Kentucky." He then reached around her shoulders and gently pulled her body close to his and said, "I'll be back in the spring to marry you and take you with me to our new home in Kentucky." He then forced a smile on his troubled face and said, "Can you wait, honey?"

She looked at him with tears rolling down her cheeks and said, "If I can't, I'll come to you."

The harvest went very fast for the Cooper's as it did for the rest of the planters in the area. Each day began at sun up and they didn't return to their little slave cabins until sun down. There was no time for socializing so Mark and Sarah didn't see much of each other except in church on Sunday mornings.

Some how Mark had found time to practice his new sport of cracking his fathers legendary black whip. He also began to notice the slaves were watching him more and talking to him less. This troubled him at first as he seen the black families he grew up with still speak to him and show respect for his authority but not stopping to chat with him like they use to when he was young. Mark began to realize that his father was right. If you do own and work slaves, to protect your authority and investment you must install into their minds the element of fear while displaying a since of compassion that they can see and feel but never quite touch. For the first time Mark realized his father was not only a master with the long black whip, but also in displaying that sense of compassion to his slaves that some how filled the void for their desire to be free.

Chapter Fifteen
Mark Prepares to Leave for Kentucky

The harvest was now coming to and end and the festivals were about to begin in the little country town. Sunday morning found Mark and Sarah setting together in church. After the services they walked out together holding hands and were meet by Mr. and Mrs. Howiton who were waiting for them to come out.

They invited Mark to come out to the house for dinner and as they turned to leave Mr. Howiton turned back to Mark and said, "I've got something I want to talk to you about."

Mark replied "Sarah and I will be there shortly." Mark then turned to his father and asked, "Can I borrow your buggy for a while?"

His father replied, "Yes," as he grinned, and said, "I guess that means I have to go home in the wagon, doesn't it."

Mark put his hand on his father's shoulder and said, "Look at it this way, Dad, now you can see what the best looking buggy in the county looks like from a distance."

Everybody in the churchyard waved as Mark and Sarah drove way. They were still looking and chatting with each other as they saw Sarah slide over and put her head on Mark's shoulder as their buggy slowly disappeared into the beauty of the Virginia hills.

After their dinner was over, Mr. Howiton said to Mark, "Son, I've been wanting to talk to you by yourself for quite some time now. The reason being I'd like to know a little bit about this place called Kentucky that you seem to be so fond of."

Mark seemed surprised as he looked at Sarah and over to her father. He then said, "Well, sir, what would you like to know about it?"

"Well," he said, "is there really a large number of families traveling west through the Gap like we're hearing about, or is it more people like you seeking adventure?"

"Well, sir," Mark replied, "there's a lot of both. For example," he said, "you have a lot of families going west in search of land and you have a lot of people following the trails to provide services that might be needed by the families on the way." He then grinned and said, "Of course, there's always the hunters and mountain men like Big Sean Davies that seem to put the glamor in the stories of the wild west."

Sarah and her mother had went into the kitchen to do the dishes when Mr. Howiton slid over close to Mark and said in a low voice, "I've been thinking about going west to look for some of that land that everybody's been talking about."

"I hear," he went on to say, "you are planning on leaving to go back out west shortly. Is that true?"

"Yes, sir, I am."

Mr. Howiton said, "Well, I can't go now, but if you don't mind would you draw me a detailed map on how to get to where you are planning to settle."

"Yes, sir, I can, but I must warn you that there can be a lot of hardships in the wilderness land west of the Gap."

"I know, Mark, but can you draw it up for me while the girls are in the kitchen?" asked Mr. Howiton.

"Yes," replied Mark as he took the paper from him and drew him a route to follow and told him some places to stay over at night.

About that time Sarah and her mother came out of the kitchen with the desert ready to serve. After visiting for a while Mark and Sarah both new that a stroll in the afternoon would be to tempting so he said his goodbyes as he left with Sarah to walk out to the buggy. Sarah's mom and dad were watching through a crack in the curtain as they seen them embrace each other for a long period of time.

Mr. Howiton looked at Sarah's mother and said, "You know our daughter can't wait that long and that boy knows it."

She replied with a sad look on her face, "Yes, I know."

He took her hand and said, "You know I have to admire that boy very much for the sacrifice he's about to make to make sure her and our wishes are honored."

After their embrace Mark stepped into the buggy as he turn and looked into her beautiful blue eyes for the last time for serval months and said, "I'll see you in the spring next year, honey."

The sun was about half way from noon to the blue ridge on its daily afternoon trip as Sarah watched the buggy disappear into the rolling country side.

The next morning while at the breakfast table Mark informed his mother and father of his intension.

They both were quit for a short time and then his father said, "Well, I guess if you must go it's best you go before the weather changes to much."

His mother said, "Before you go get with me as I want to send a little something with you for Willie."

Mark replied by saying, "I'll be leaving Sunday morning early, that should give me time to finish up our loose ends here on the farm and still allow me time to pack for the trip."

The week went fast and Sunday morning found Mark climbing up on his horse and waving goodbye to his family and slaves that had gathered to see him off.

As he turned his horse to leave Willie's Mom ran over from the crowd grabbed his leg and said "Master Mark, sir, please tell our son how much we love him and miss him!"

Mark replied, "I will, Mamie, but I'm sure he already knows that." When Mark reached the top of the hill that offered a view of the big house and the little slave cabins he stopped turned in his saddle and looked back down. There he seen the memories of his childhood days pass before his eyes as it drew into his mind a picture view of the past that would be handed down for the generation to remember.

Chapter Sixteen
Mark Leaves to Build Sarah a Home

In less than two weeks later Mark was going through the Cumberland Gap when he stopped his horse to rest He turned in his saddle to look back into Virginia mountains and thought to himself how great it would be if only Sarah was with him. He then turned back around and looked to the west at the majestic view before his eyes and said out loud, "It's good to be home."

Four days later at twelve noon there was a knock on the door of a little log cabin now the home of the Morgan family. When Bill Morgan opened the door Mark Cooper could smell the aroma of a home cooked meal and heard the familiar voice say, "You're just in time for dinner, Mark." After handshakes and hugs they all sat down to eat. Mark complemented Mrs. Morgan on the food and said, "My goodness, you folks have done a lot of work in a short period of time."

Bill laughed and said, "Well, Mark, we can't take all the credit for it as that Willie of yours and Big Sean helped us about every day for a long time after you were gone."

"What happened to Eli?" Mark asked.

"Well," Bill said, "he was helping, too, but said they would have to leave so they could get their land cleared and cabin built before the bad whether set in. Before he left he said to tell you that you could find them by going to the settlement of Russellville and inquiring at the local store there."

"Oh, by the way, Mark, how's that Sarah of yours doing?" asked Mrs. Morgan.

"She's doing find now," Mark replied. Then he told her how serious her condition was, but didn't dwell on why he left sooner than planned.

Bill said, "I thought you was going to stay and help your father until next spring when you would marry Sarah and then come back out here."

"Well," Mark said, "we're still planning on getting married next spring, but when we got pretty well done with the harvest I had the urge to come on out and maybe try to prepare a home for us to live in after we're married."

"Oh," Bill said, "before I forget it, I've got a map that Big Sean drew for you to use to find them."

Mark displayed his thin smile and asked, "By the way, have them two stayed out of trouble?"

Bill looked at his wife and they both laughed as he said, "You know it's kinda hard for those two to stay out of trouble." He then said, "Let's put it this way, no one in that town will be giving Willie trouble anymore!"

Mark spent the next day with Mr Morgan as they looked at some of the things that they had done to prepare his land so they could start the process of planting for the following year. They ended the day by looking at the land that Mark was the owner of.

He seemed very pleased, but looked at Bill with a grin and said, "I'd like to stay the winter here, but something tells me I need to go on west and check on Willie and Big Sean."

Bill looked at Mark with a more serious look and said, "If it's any ease to your mind, he didn't have Willie doing any arm wrestling while they were in this area that I've heard of anyway."

"That's good to hear," replied Mark as he turn to walk back to the log cabin to eat super.

At the super table they all talked an laughed about the adventures they had going out west in the presence of a wild roaring mountain man and a muscle bound starry eyed slave boy. When the laughing died down Mark got up to go bed down for the night as he looked at the Morgan family and said, "You know Willie always wanted to go west and leave a mark for others to follow." Then with a thin smile on his face, he said, "Maybe that's just what their doing."

Mark was awoke the next morning by a familiar sound of a roster outside his window as he laid there for a few minutes thinking of his home in Virginia, his land in Kentucky and his dream of free land in Illinois. He soon found himself at the breakfast table as he talked to Bill about farming his land for him if he didn't get back to farm it him self in the spring. They sealed the agreement with a hand shake and Mark left within the hour.

The trail was easy to find from the map that Mark used but he really didn't need it, as the stories about a roaring mountain man and a muscular slave boy traveling through the countryside a few weeks back were circulating about every where he stopped. The sun was about to set a few days later as Mark tied the reins of Apple Bee's bridle to the hitching post in front a little store in the settlement of Russellville Kentucky.

Inside the store, Mark asked the owner if he new or heard of Big Sean Davis and a slave boy named Willie.

The owner laughed and said, "Who hasn't?"

Mark introduced himself to the owner and stated, "That Willie was his slave and Big Sean a good friend of his."

The owner introduced himself as Paul Friend.

When they were shaking hands Mark grinned and said, "It might be good to know a friend in this wilderness country, wouldn't you say, sir?"

He laughed and replied, "It is unless you want to live like a mountain man."

"Speaking of mountain men how's that Big Sean and my slave boy doing?"

"They were in town last weekend and didn't get into any trouble for a change," replied Paul, the store owner, "so I guess that's a good sign they're doing okay. He then stopped and looked Mark over from head to toe," and said, "I'll say one thing about those two, they done a very good job of describing their boss man to me. I think I would have known you even if you hadn't stopped in."

"What kinda trouble have those two been getting into?" asked Mark as a smile began to appear on his lips.

"Well, you know when you got a big roaring mountain man and a musclebound slave boy coming to town it draws a lot of attention to begin with," replied Paul. Then he said, "On top of that, there's the story going around about this Willie boy of yours being the best arm wrestler in the west." He looked at Mark, grinned, and said, "And that's when the trouble starts!"

"What do you mean by that?" asked Mark as his smile turned into a more concerned look.

"Well, sir, you're in the wild west out here. Young bucks don't have a whole lot of social activity in their lives, so when they do come to town and see a black slave boy getting all the attention it starts getting under their skin. Then, of course, it doesn't help when the boy won't take them on in a contest. So they start calling him names and before you know it that big wild mountain man is knocking people down faster than they can get up." Paul took time out to shake his head and laugh and said, "Then that Willie boy starts helping him out."

Mark grinned and said, "Why doesn't Willie just arm wrestle the men and get it over with?"

Paul replied, "I think you know the anser to that, sir, since you were the one who gave the order to that big man; no arm wrestling while I'm gone, and sealed it with a handshake." Paul saw the concerned look on Mark's face and said, "When two men in this part of the country seal an agreement with a handshake it's the same as a legal binding agreement, which is honored and respected."

"I know," replied Mark as he thought for a moment and said to Paul, "Maybe it's time for me to go have a talk with them."

"They're out at the Elie Cox place," said Paul, "and if you'll wait a moment I'll draw you a map on how to get there."

As he handed Mark the map he grinned and said, "I think Elie's is going to be glad to see you."

IN SEARCH OF FREE LAND

About a half hour later Mark stopped again to look at his map to where the *X* was marked on the paper. Then as he looked at the country side before him he saw a log cabin. There was smoke rasing from the chimney of the little cabin and he could see some other log buildings in the process of being built. When Mark looked down at the view before him he thought to himself this could very well be the first place I put down some roots.

He then turned in his saddle and looked back to the east as if to be talking to Sarah and said, "I hope you like it, honey." When he reached the cabin Mark could smell the aroma of home cooking filtering through his nostrils, causing him to pound on the door and say, as loud as he could, "You got any food in there for a beggar?"

The door opened and there, before his eyes, stood two hundred or more pounds of black sunshine that seemed to glow as he shouted, "Master Mark's here!"

The smell of that good food filtering through the cabin had to wait as handshakes and hugs took center stage. A few minutes later, Willie was carrying in from the outside a log the right height to be a chair for Mark to set at the humble table of Eli Cox. Big Sean and Willie had just gotten back from a short hunting trip so there was an abundance of food on the table. Of course, everyone wanted to know all about Mark's trip back home, why he was back so soon and what happened to Sarah. Mark answered each question, one at a time, in between the sampling of the game that was cooked to perfection and could have curled the taste buds of the most elite among men. The conversation had brought everyone up to date on what had happened the last few months as the supper meal came to and end. Mark stopped eating not because of the like of food but for the need to make room for desert that he seen already waiting to be served by Mrs. Cox over by the fire place. He then asked to be excused, as he stood up he realized how small the cabin was. He noticed that it was one room with a loft on each end. He also noticed that there appeared to be just enough room for his family to sleep. He then walked over and looked up at the sleeping area. Then as he turned back to Eli he asked, "Is that your sleeping quarters?"

Eli replied, "Yes, it is, Mark," and then he said, "it would have been smaller than this if it hadn't been for Big Sean and that Willie boy of yours helping so much." He looked at both men in admiration and said because they helped in building shelters for the animals we now have time to clear some land for farming before the winter set in.

After the meal was over and desert had been served Mark complemented Mrs. Cox on the excellences of the food. Then he said as he looked around the table at everyone, I'm sorry I wasn't here to help you through all of the hardships you must have endured.

Mrs. Cox was the first to reply as she said, "No, Mark, your Sarah was more important at the time."They all nodded their heads in agreement as she said, "Just think what might have happened if you hadn't gone back."

Mark looked at each person at that humble table and said, "In the short time I was gone you were able to by the swing of your axes, the blast of your guns and maybe a fight or two alone the way notch a path into the wilderness land of Kentucky for others to follow." Mark then looked over and said with a smile that was getting close to a large grin, "Now as far as you two are concerned, I believe it's time we unseal our agreement about arm wrestling while I was gone."

Big Sean rubbed Willie kinky black hair and said with a roaring voice, "Does that mean your boy can go to town with me Saturday."

Mark, with a grin still on his face, replied, "I expect the both of you to go to town and answer any unanswered questions that may be floating around." With his face taking on a more serious look, he said, "I may just go with you to witness the occasion."

The evening came to an end with Mark bedding down on a straw tick that was used for a mattress. Two of the Cox children gave up their bed for the opportunity to sleep in the uncompleted barn with Willie and Big Sean.

The next few days Mark got a real feel of the hardships involved in attempting to plant roots in the untamed frontier land of Kentucky. Mark agreed to help Eli while Big Sean and Willie finished up the log building that would house the horses, cows and chickens that Eli had already purchased in town the last time.

Saturday came at last for Mark and as he attempted to clean up he realized how serious the blisters on his hands were from the hours of swing the axe to down the trees and notch the logs. He then remembered Willie and Big Sean as they rased the large logs above their heads to set them in place for Eli to mortar them together. He looked again at his blistered hands and said to himself, "To complain about this after what they been through would be shameful." Mark walked out into the yard and there stood Big Sean and Willie, a thin smile came across his lips as he noticed Willie wearing a large, oversized shirt.

Mark rased his arm up above his head and said, "Come on, boys, let's go to town and have some fun."

It was a warm mid afternoon in early October as the three horsemen road down a narrow dirt path called a street to a few buildings that appeared to be the gathering point for the small settlement of Russellville, Kentucky. One of the buildings was that of Paul Friend who owned the store where Mark had stopped a few days earlier.

As the three horsemen dismounted, Mark said, "Willie, you'll be going with me to the store."

Willie replied, "Yes, sir, Master Mark."

Big Sean said, "I'll see you boys later. I got me a powerful thirst to quench."

After visiting with Paul Friend, Mark placed an order for some stable supplies, including cornmeal, flour, sugar, and said, "We'll be back to pick them up before we leave town." Then they left the little store and walked down to the main gathering point, the local tavern.

Mark looked over at Willie and grinned as he asked, "Do you think Big Sean might be in there?"

Willie's grin turned into a large smile as he said, "I think he probably is, Master Mark."

"Let's find out," replied Mark as he pushed the door open and heard the noise in the room turn completely silent. The man behind the bar was the first to speak as he looked at Big Sean standing in front of him and Mark over by the door and Willie by his side. He raised his arm up and said, "Now, gentlemen, I don't want any trouble in here."

Mark made a few steps toward the bar as Willie follow behind. Mark by now was within eye contact of the bartender. His black eyes seemed to snap as he said, "We will honor and respect your authority in your own place of business, sir, but I would think as a gentleman you would not deny the patrons of your fine establishment the opportunity to witness for a few minutes such an occasion."

"Everybody by now had heard all about the arm wrestling stories of a roaring mountain man, a muscular slave boy and a tall, snappy-eyed Virginia planter."

Before Earl the bartender could say a word Big Sean was waving his large arm above his head saying, "Come on, boys, let's give Earl boy here a hand."

By now Earl was cleaning a table for the contest to take place.

Big Sean said, "Come on, boys, line up so you can take on the best in the west."

The line was starting to grow until Willie removed his large oversized shirt and then it started getting smaller as they began to change their minds as they looked across the table at the muscular black body of the slave boy with whip marks across his back.

One big white boy didn't seem to be intimidated by the size of the large arms of Willie as he sat down across the table from him and said, "Okay, boy, let's see what you got."

The boy appear to between eighteen and twenty years of age and from his tall lanky body hung two large arms with hands as big as Big Sean's. When they put their arms on the table Willie realized the boys arm was longer then his and it might put him at a disadvantage. Willie new by now if he was going to win this one it would have to happen in the first split second after the count. Three was still ring in the air from the roaring voice of Big Sean as the long lanky arm of the white boy moved ever so slowly downward toward the table. Willie new he had got the break but would have to use every muscle in his body to finish it fast because he felt this white boy would display to much holding power for him to overcome. About that time Big Sean roared out in a voice that seem to shake the room by saying, "Now, boy, now!"

IN SEARCH OF FREE LAND

Wilbur the big white boy flinched from the roar of the voice and it may have given Willie the opportunity he needed for the arm of Wilbur began to move downward more rapidly until all of a sudden it slammed against the table with such force that it was heard all the way across the room.

Wilbur reacted different then the rest of the men Willie had defeated in the past. He just sat there and appeared to be lost for words.

After a few seconds he looked up at Willie who was standing by then and said, "have you ever done any log splitting boy?

Willie replied by saying, "Yes, Master Wilbur, sir. But I can tell," he said, "you have done a lot more than I have."

Wilbur was standing by then as he said, "What makes you think that, boy?"

Again Willie replied with respect as he said, "Well, sir, my hand is still numb and my shoulder fells like its been pulled out of its socket." Willie then released his trademark big smile as his shiny white teeth seemed to glow between his rounded coal black cheeks.

Wilbur started laughing as he put his hand out to shook Willie's hand and said, "You beat me fair and square, boy!" He then rubbed Willie's black kinky hair and said, "I'd like to make a rail splitter out of you."

Willie, still smiling, said, "And I'd like to make an arm wrestler out of you."

Big Sean had done collected the winnings and was up at the bar ordering drinks for everyone. Mark was observing Wilbur and Willie to make sure no conflict developed as he over heard their conversation.

He then stepped in closer to them and said to Wilbur, "My name is Mark Cooper and I'm looking for a good log splitter. Are you available?"

Wilbur put his hand out to shake Marks hand and replied, "It's a privilege to meet you, sir."

A grin appeared below his stern looking gray eyes as he said, "I've heard a lot about you, your guide and slave boy here. In anser to your question, sir. Yes, I'm available. But just how long would it last?"

Mark's thin smile exposed itself again as he said, "Well, if you and my boy, Willie, here can get alone, okay, it could be for a long time."

Late that night the party of three that came through the Cumberland Gap together now became a party of four. The room where they stayed that night was casting a small beam of light through a crack in between the logs in the little log building that was used to house four horses and one cow. There on a bed of straw laid the four men in the log barn of Eli Cox. This would be their home until the log cabin of Marks was completed. Shortly that beam of light moved on to the eyes of Willie.

Then Big Sean and Wilbur started laughing as Wilbur said, "I see two eyes and no body!"

About that time Willie jumped up and grab Wilbur and said, "Got you, white boy!"

Mark could then be heard as he said, "Okay, boys, before this spook stuff goes to fair I expect three bodies and six eyes looking at me all in one peace at the break of dawn in the morning."

The next morning they awoke to some sounds out side and as they walked out of the barn there was six men waiting to help then build the house for Mark. They were present in town when Willie and Wilbur were the center of attraction. They told Mark they had heard about the three men from Virginia and wanted to offer their labor for a few days.

Mark accepted their offer and said, "I would like to invite you in for some breakfast, but I would have to ask permission from the four horses and one cow first."

They all laughed and said, "You probably wouldn't get it anyway. So," they said, "what can we do to get started?"

Mark replied by saying, "Well, for starters, you can shake hands with my guide, Big Sean Davis, my slave boy, Willie, and, of course, you probably already no Wilbur here." With a big smile on his face he said, "You know Big Sean here is one of the best cooks between here and the Blue Ridge and I bet he'd like it if you all chipped in and helped him set up a temporary kitchen right under those trees over there. Remember," he said with a chuckle, "being friends with the cook is pretty important when you been cutting and splitting logs all day."

They all agreed one hundred percent. Then they all walked over and said, "Where do we start, big boy."

The little cabin that was to be the home for Mark and Sarah seemed to go up over night but of course it was serval days. Big Sean had to take a leave of absents a couple of times to go into the near by woods and bring back food for the table. The cabin was all most done to the point that they could move in and the men that had came to helped had left. There was a bed and dresser in the bed room that Mark had purchased in town from a family that couldn't handle the hardships of the rugged frontier. The kitchen area had moved from under the trees to the second room of the cabin. There was plans being made to build a smaller cabin about twenty feet from the present one with a roof between the two. It then some day would become their guest room, but for the present it would be Willie and Big Sean's room.

One day Willie was outside of the cabin when he seen a strange looking buggy coming down the path that by now was being used as a road. He stood and watch for a moment and then yelled Mark, Mark, come here! Mark came out of the cabin as Willie said, "Over there, coming down the road." Mark's black eyes was observing the seen as he saw a horse pulling a black buggy with a top on it. He notice there was a black driver in front and there appeared to be a man and a lady in the back seat. As the buggy got closer Mark's hart began to beat so hard that the blood rushing to his head caused him to turn his eyes away in disbelief. When he turned his head back the image was clear and Mark new beyond a doubt it was his beloved Sarah. Willie new by now from the reaction of Mark that it had to be Sarah. He then grabbed a hold of the bridle on the horse that was tied to the hitching rail.

When Mark turn to tell him who was there Willie handed the reins to Mark and said, "Here you are, sir." Mark jumped up on Apple Bee and in a dead run they approached the buggy coming up to the cabin. Apple Bee was even with the horse pulling the buggy when Mark jumped off and reached up as Sarah stood up. He then pulled her down from the buggy into his arms. The buggy was by now stopped as Mr. Howiton leaned over to observe with a smile his daughter in the arms of her lover and soon to be husband. Her feet were dangling a few inches above the ground from the grip of his strong arms as he pulled her tender body in close to his. There eyes looked deep into each other for the first time in serval weeks. There was no need for words as their lips came together gently at first and then with more force until the soft body of Sarah gave in completely to the commands of the ridged body of Mark.

When they came up for air the first one to speak was Mark as he asked, "Why are you here?"

Sarah said with a smile, "do you remember when you asked me if I would wait for you and I said I would if I could." She reached up and ran her fingers through his hair as she looked deep into his coal black eyes and said with a tear in her eyes, "Well, I couldn't."

A thin smile appeared on Mark's face as he said, "I am so glad you couldn't."

Sarah's father had done stepped down from the buggy so Mark and Sarah could ride up to their new Kentucky home in style. Willie was waiting at the door when they pulled up in front. He reached up and took Sarah's hand and helped her down from the fancy buggy. When her feet touched the ground she put her arms around his neck and gave him a hug and said, "It's so good to see you, Willie."

Willie's emotional smile turned into a large grin as he walked over to the cabin door opened it and said, "May I ask who's calling, ma'am?"

With a small grin on her face she said, "Mr. And Mrs. Cooper."

"Please enter," replied Willie as his attempt to keep a straight face gave way to an even larger smile.

As they interred the cabin Mark said, "Willie, will you go take care of the driver and buggy?"

"I sure will, Master Mark, sir," replied Willie as he left the cabin.

Mr. Howiton was just coming up the path to the cabin as Big Sean came out of the near by woods with game for the evening meal. In a little over an hour a meal fit for a king was cooked by Big Sean and served by Willie and the driver to Sarah, Mark and her father. After considerable coaching from Sarah, Big Sean Willie and the driver sat down at the table made from logs in cabin nested in the wilderness land of Kentucky. It would be the first of many meals that would be served in what was soon to be the home of Sarah and Mark Cooper. Willie had just said, "Please pass the meat," when a knock came from the door of the cabin. Mark asked Willie to anser the door and see who was there. When Willie opened the door a tall lanky man with a well groomed beard came through the door carrying a black book in his hand that appeared to be a bible.

He introduced himself as Reverend Springer and said, "I have just come from the Eli Cox place and he said he thought you had your cabin about finished. So I thought I'd come over and personally welcome you to the territory as a new home owner."

Mark stood up and said, "Thank you so much, Reverend Springer, and now I'd like to introduce you to my wife-to-be and her father." After the handshakes, Mark said, "I think you already know Willie and Big Sean here."

Reverend Springer laughed and said, "Who don't know those two rascals."

Mark said, "Won't you stay and have dinner with us?"

"I would be pleased to, but it looks to me like you got a full table already, Mark."

Mark replied back to the reverend by saying, "There will always be a spot at our are table for you, sir."

He then reached down to take Sarah hand who was by now rasing from her log called a chair to stand by her man. Willie and the driver of Mr. Howiton buggy were already up from the table so the reverend Springer could set down. Willie and the other slave were leaving the room carrying some food on a plank of wood as the reverend Springer said, "Bless you, boys."

The reverend gave the blessing for the food and as they were eating he said, "Mark, I hear you and Sarah are planning on getting married soon."

Mark and Sarah looked at each other and then over to her father, both with a big smile on their face. Mr. Howiton picked up on the emotion as they looked at each other and said, "Now wait a minute, kids." He saw the glow in their eyes and new these two could not be apart as he said, "Sarah, you know your mother wanted me to make sure you got a proper wedding."

Sarah put her arms around her father who was sitting next to her and said, "Daddy, I love you and Mother so very much. But the circle of my life now as expanded to include Mark, the love of my life. He is now the man I wish to spend the rest of my days on earth with, starting today."

Mark was holding Sarah's hand as he said, "Reverend Springer, sir, would you and could you marry us today?"

The reverend looked over to Sarah's father who was by now in deep thought and said, "Of course I can, Mark."

Mark then said, "Father," as he looked over at Mr. Howiton and asked, "would you give me your daughter's hand in marriage with your and Mother's blessing?"

Sarah's father raised his head and wiped a tear from his eyes as he said, "Yes, I will, but only if we attempt to follow her mother's and Mrs. Cooper's wishes."

In a few minutes the little log cabin began to look like a church with the table across the back of the room and split logs setting on log cut offs on each side of the room leaving an ale down the middle of the little room. Big Sean went out and brought Willie and the driver in to witness the wedding that was about to take place. The reverend Springer was on the back side of the table facing the door and Mark stood facing him on the front side of the table. Big Sean was setting on one side of the ale and the driver sitting on the other side. The reverend gave Willie the signal and watched as he walled over and open the door to the cabin and escorted Mr. Howiton and his daughter Sarah down the make shift ale pass Big Sean and the driver then when Sarah was even with Mark they stopped.

The reverend Springer then asked, "Who gives this lady in marriage?

Her father replied by saying, "Her mother and I."

He then walk back and sat on the side of the ale behind his daughter. The weeding began with Willie sitting behind Big Sean, on one side of the ale and Mr. Howiton sitting in front of his driver on the other side.

The reverend looked out across the room as if it was a large church and said, "Isn't the imagination a wonderful thing." He then preformed the ceremony and said, "I now pronounce you man and wife." They were looking deep into each other's eyes with smiles on their faces when they heard the words, "You may now kiss the bride." Sarah's toes were barely touching the dirt floor inside the log cabin as her lips came in contact with Mark's. Then as their lips searched deeper to overcome the idle contentment of two people deeply in love, a shadow of a picture in their minds was cast, not of a log cabin in the middle of the Kentucky wilderness, but of a castle in a place called Paradise.

When Sarah's lips parted from Mark's and her feet fell upon the solid ground inside the log cabin, Mark's thin smile appeared as he said, "Honey, if a home is a man's castle then welcome to our castle!"

After the hugs and congratulation Sarah's father had his driver to go with him out to the buggy and when they returned the driver had a saddle bag hanging on his shoulder. Sarah's father was caring a black leather case that he laid down and took two envelopes from the saddle bag hanging on the drivers shoulders.

He then handed one envelope to Mark and said, "Your father and mother wanted you to have this." Mark open the envelope and there was a bank note mark paid in full and signed by Will Cooper for the purchase of one slave named Willie. Sarah's father then handed the second envelope to Sarah and said, "Your mother and Mrs. Cooper wanted you to have this." It was a letter saying, "We love you Mrs. Cooper and the furniture for your new home will be coming soon."

A tear was dripping from Sarah's eyes as her father put his arms around her shoulders and said, "I love you, too, honey." He then turn back to Mark and said oh by the way Mark your father wanted you to have this also as he picked up the black leather case and handed it to Mark. Mark took the case then reached inside it and pulled out a long black whip. A note was attach to it saying as you go in your search for free land use this sparingly and wisely and let us hope that it may some day be retired and remembered as only a "legend of past."

The sun by now had began to hide it's face behind the trees in the wilderness forest to the west allowing the newly weds the privacy they so desperately needed. The glow left by the setting sun offered a view that seemed to high light the image of a black buggy being pulled by a black horse carrying Sarah's father and his driver down a path called a road away from the little log cabin. Behind them was a horse carrying the reverend Springer and down by the cabin two large men were walking, one white, one black, to a shelter now being used as a place to sleep for the night. The glow from the setting sun then dissipated into the dark of night as the dime light in the bed room of the little log cabin offered the only indication of life in the valley below. The light soon went out being replace by the rhythmic sounds of contentment riding the breezes of the midnight air. Sometime before the first light of dawn, peace fell upon the valley as the calm breeze of the late night morning carried from the cabin window ever so gently the faint words, "I love you." This feeling of two people desperately in love would be remembered of a little log cabin known as their castle, in a place called "paradise."

The sun rose from hiding and peaked it's smiling face into the open window of the little log cabin and awoke from a contented sleep the father and mother of the next generation of the Cooper family.

In the months to follow the place they wants called paradise finally became reality as they struggled like most other families to carve out a home in the wilderness land of Kentucky.

Chapter Seventeen
Prosperous Days on the Frontier

Their furniture from Virginia had finally arrived and the log cabin was starting to look like a real home after the finishing touches from Sarah's were put in place. Willie was being keep buses helping clear land for both Mark and Eli Cox. Big Sean was becoming restless and one day after a hunting trip told Mark the time had come for him to head back home to Virginia. After the hand shakes and hugs Mark and Sarah turned toward the cabin with a sad feeling in their harts. Then they heard a roaring sound and turned back to see what was going on, when they saw the large arms of the mighty mountain man go around the big black shoulders of Willie and squeezed so hard that his feet came off the ground.

Then with a roaring laugh that seemed to vibrate the moist air from the morning dew he said that's for that bear that didn't get to give you a bear hug back there in the blue ridge mountains. "Do you remember that boy?" He asked as he reached up and grab the saddle horn.

"How could I not remember," said Willie with a big grin as a tear fell on his big black cheeks.

Big Sean then climbed upon his horse, looked down at Willie and said, "The next time we meet I'll expect you to be strong enough to take on the big man himself in an arm wrestling contest."

Willie's grin had left his face as he watch the man he idealized ride off to the east. He shook his head and said, "I doubt that, Master Sean."

Mark and Sarah's short love a fair would soon be tested for longevity by the wondering feet of Mark Cooper. Within a year he was looking for land to the south that would soon become Simpson County near a settlement called Franklin. He had acquired a few slaves by then and had begun to clear land for farming.

Two years later the fruits of their labor began to payoff. From the harvest of their crops and furs from the nearby timbers they loaded their wagons and began their trip to a river to the west and north. There they built a flat bottom boat from the available trees that were close to the river. When the boat was loaded a neighbor paid Mark for some of the horses and wagons. With the help of Mark's slaves he drove the wagons back to his place to be refilled again. Then Mark, Willie and Wilbur stepped upon the boat and with a long pole pushed off and began their first floating trip down a stream that would take them to the Ohio and then to the mighty Mississippi to a place called New Orleans. The freedom feelings of the flowing rivers and the classy atmosphere of New Orleans appeared to be the fulfilling need for the Virginia planter and the starry eyed slave boy. During their trip the trio left their mark when they stopped at different places alone the way. By the time they reached New Orleans there were tales of a muscle-bound slave boy arm wrestler, a powerful ax man named Wilbur and a snappy-eyed Virginia planter that gave demonstrations to show how deadly accurate he could be with his long black whip. With the money from the horses and wagons he sold where they began their trip they were able two by two horses and a wagon for the trip back to Kentucky. Then with the money he got from the goods he took to New Orleans and the money from the people that rode back north in the wagon with him Mark had turned a sizeable profit in his third full year of farming the wilderness land of Kentucky.

The first night back in their little log cabin his vivid memories of the peaceful rolling, endless waters of the Mississippi would soon give way to the rhythmic sounds of contentment once again riding the breeze of the midnight air.

The next morning the rising sun awoke two people still passionately in love looking deep into each others eyes as Mark said, "Sarah, honey, can we call him William?"

As she ran her fingers through his black, wavy hair she said, "I think he'd like that, dear." She then smiled and said, "That is if it's a boy."

He returned to her an oversized thin smile as he pulled her soft desirable looking body in close to his and said, "I generally get what I want."

She haft heartedly pushed back and said, "I've been noticing that." The word *that* was still slipping through her lips as her arms pulled the stiffest part of his rigid body even closer to hers. And then another night in Paradise came to an end.

Nine months later, a boy named William was born in the wilderness of Kentucky to the Cooper family. As the boy opened his eyes to look at the new world, his father looked at his mother with that smile on his face and said, "Didn't I tell you I always get what I want?"

The year was 1813 and Mark was doing well in the farming business. He had made two more trips to New Orleans and was starting to be thought of by his neighbors as a man of importance. One day he said to Sarah, "Don't you think its about time for our young ones to see their grandpa and grandma?"

Her big blue eyes beamed with delight as she swing her arms around his neck and said, "Can we take Willie with us?"

Mark grinned and said, "Of course we can, a lady of your stature in the community must have a servant when you travel."

The next few days went fast as they prepared to leave their home in the wilderness land of Kentucky for their first trip back to Virginia.

Chapter Eighteen
Willie Becomes a Free Man

Travel in the early 1800s was hard and only done under necessity. So to see a family traveling with servants would of course draw attention. There were still stories floating around as they traveled east about men from Virginia a few years back that included a snappy-eyed Virginia planter, a starry eyed muscular slave boy and a wild mountain man named Big Sean. The rumors indicated that Big Sean was now down in Tennessee and some rumors placed him in the mountains west of the Mississippi.

After what seemed like a lifetime, they found themselfs on a high point east of the blue ridge, looking down at a place they once called home.

Their visit was coming to an end with only one day left when Will and Mrs. Cooper invited Willie and his mom and dad to come to the big house for a farewell dinner. After he said the blessing, Will Cooper said to all at the table, "My son has an announcement to make."

Mark stood up and said to Willie, "You have been a loyal servant to both my father and me and have stood with me through the hardship of the frontier as we together cut a path through the wilderness land for others to follow." He then reached into his pocket and took out a folded paper, unfolded it and handed it to Willie. He than asked Willie to read the contents to everyone at the table. When he got to the part that said you are now a free man, tears of joy were flowing down the deep black cheeks of his mom and dad. When the dessert was served, Willie asked if he could give the blessing again?

Will nodded his head and said, "Okay, Willie."

Willie then gave the blessing the way he was taught by his master Will when he was a little boy.

As he raised his head and wiped a tear from his stern looking face Will Cooper said to Willie, "Now that you are a free man my God be with you where ever you go and in whatever you do."

Mark winked at Sarah with a devilish look as he then turned to Willie and said, "Now that you are free will you be going west with us or will you be staying here with your family?"

Willie looked over at his mom and dad and then over to the man that had once spared his life at the end of a long black whip. He thought for a moment and said, "I've only been free for a few minutes and already I'm having to make a decision that I wouldn't have to make if I was still a slave. But now that I am free, I know I must follow my hart, that is now calling me back beyond the blue ridge to the land I love so much." Willie then looked at Mark and Sarah and said, "Can I still be your servant on the way back home?"

Everyone at the table began laughing at Willie's sincere question as they finished their desert.

Their visit ended the next day in the church yard with their friends, neighbors and family all waving goodbye. The grandparents were all waiving at their grandchildren being carried away in a wagon that was pulled by two horses and driven by a free black man as they wondered if they would ever see them again.

Chapter Nineteen
The Exploratory Trip to the Illinois Territory

The next few years slowly passed by as the wondering feet of Mark's began to itch. He had heard stories about the land north of the Ohio and east of the Mississippi. The stories described large wagons with white covered tops called prairie ships. They were called that because from a distance they looked like ships on an ocean as they traveled through the tall grasses of the endless prairie. They were used to carry settlers to the new land that would soon be the State of Illinois. Some were called squatters. They were men with wondering feet that would take advantage of the free land until the next frontier opened up. These settlers and squatters would settle in small communities generally near water and some timber. They would then venture out into the prairie and try to farm it. They of course didn't have tools and equipment to farm the mass amount of land that was available for their taking. Mark couldn't take it anymore, he had to go see this land where the grass looked like the mighty oceans. Sarah didn't want Mark to go but knew she wouldn't be able to change his mind so she agreed to see to it with the help of some neighbors, their kids and a few slaves that the crops got planted and attended to while he was gone.

Mark called Willie in from the fields and said, "Willie, how would like to go with me north to the land between the rivers where the grass grows taller the then a man and the large wagons with white covered tops appear as ships on an ocean."

A smile appeared on his black rounded face that exposed his brilliant white teeth as he said, "Yes, sir, Master Mark, sir!"

Willie had been free for a long time by now but was still working for Mark and the Cox family most of the time. He was also one of the better hunters and log splitters in the area and was able to save up a little money.

A few days later Mark and Willie found themselves on the South side of the Ohio river, looking across at a little boom town. There was a ferry boat operating there that took the people from Kentucky across the Ohio river to the little boom town now called Golconda. The town consisted of serval hundred people as it had become a refueling point for the steamers that was by then starting to appear on the Ohio and Mississippi rivers. It was also the entrance to a land route from the Ohio across Illinois to the Mississippi to another ferry boat that could take people who wished, to the land west of the river to what is now called Missouri. There were serval land trails north through the endless miles of prairie grass divided ever so often by trees alone side the creeks and small rivers. Mark and Willie loaded there horses on the ferry and hung on to the hand rail as they moved across the river to the little boom town. There they signed up with some Prairie Ships that would be going north west through timbers and rolling land and then follow the rivers north to a place that would soon become the capital of the new state of Illinois called Vandalia.

They found out it would be a few days before they could leave because of the amount of people waiting to come across the only ferry available. Willie made some extra money helping the owner of the ferry to move more people across the river and Mark took advantage of the available time to meet with a few wagon masters so that he might find some good farm land near a large river. Mark found out after a few conversations that some of the richest land in the new state lay south east of a large Indian village on the Illinois river that was about a one hundred miles north west of Vandalia. There they said, "The land was as black as Willie's face and as level as the floor of a cabin."

Mark asked Dave the wagon master that he would be traveling with how close the prairie was to the river.

"I don't really know," replied Dave, as he looked at Mark and said, "You see I've never been there yet. But most of the stories," he said, "put it about a day's ride to trade with the Indians and fur traders coming down river from the northern part of the state."

Mark looked at a crude map that Dave had handed him so he could study the territory that he was talking about.

After a few moments Mark raised his head as he looked at Dave and said, "It looks to me like this Indian village would be a good place to start a town."

"What makes you think that?" replied Dave.

"Well," Mark said, "if you look on this map it looks like there is two rivers that drain the prairies in the middle of the state into one river, the Illinois. That river flows south just north of this Indian village you been talking about." There was a gleam in his cold, black eyes as he said, "Dave, do you realize as we travel north that we my be entering the future bread basket of the world?"

"I never thought of it that way," replied Dave as he looked at the map that Mark handed him.

Mark said to Dave as he was looking at the map, "If you notice this Illinois River flows out of the grate lakes of the north to the golf in the south. So that means maybe some of the richest land in our country is only a days ride by land to reach a port where you can ship to the rest of the world by water."

Dave said with a chuckle, "If we keep talking and dreaming we might only be a day's ride to anywhere in the world."

Mark replied with a thin smile only if ships can fly.

Mark had already talked with Dave about Willie going a head with another hunter that had made the trip before so they could bring food and water back as needed to feed the party of settlers and squatters as they would slowly move north through the tall grasses of the prairies. The sun was getting low in the west as the two men caught a whiff of the aroma filtering up from a wagon below.

Dave looked at Mark and said, "After all that traveling you been doing today you might want to take time to get a bite to eat down at the chuck wagon."

Mark replied by saying, "It sounds like a good idea and after we eat maybe you can find the time to join me at the local pub for drink."

Dave laughed and said, "All that traveling can wear one down so maybe a good, stiff drink is just what we need."

Willie was invited to eat at one of the tables by someone he helped across the river earlier in the day. He was walking over to sit down across from the man who had invited him. Then as he set his food down on the table and started to sit down to eat, a tall, bearded man with a foul mouth grabbed his shoulder and started to pull him back. He then said in a demanding voice, "No pepper allowed at this table, boy!"

Willie put his arm out to keep the man from pulling him back as he said, "I's a free man, sir."

The bearded man replied, "I don't give a damn, boy," and started to pull harder on Willie's shoulder.

To keep from being pulled away from the table Willie shoved the man hard enough that he fell backward onto the ground. Mark and Dave were just tying their horses up close by when they seen what was going on. Mark grab the whip from his saddle just as the bearded man got up. Then the bearded man pulled a knife from his side and raised his arm to throw it at Willie. The silent's of the crowd allow the cracking sound to be heard as the tip of the long black whip rapped around the wrist of the man at the other end of it. Then the whip was jerked back causing the knife to fall to the ground.

The man started to pick up the knife when the commanding voice of Mark Harrison Cooper was heard during the silent's of the moment saying, "If you have any intention of using that hand again in the near future its best you leave that knife be. Do I make myself clear, sir?"

The bearded man looked over at Mark's cold black eyes staring at him like daggers shooting through hot metal and realized this man commanded authority. The bearded man then said, "Anything you say, sir."

Mark then looked at the people around the table and said, "Willie here," as he pointed his finger at Willie, "was my personal slave until a couple of years ago." He then said, "He gained his freedom by becoming one of the best hunters and log splitters in the state of Kentucky. He can read and write as well as anyone at this table and if he was to remove his shirt the scars on this back would indicate the price he payed for that knowledge."

Dave spoke up and said, "Willie here will be going ahead of our party with my guide and will be responsible for bringing back fresh food and water. So this might be the guy you'll want to talk to if should you have the desire some evening for a spacial dinner from the abundant hunting lands of Illinois."

Everyone at the table said at the same time, "Sit down, Willie."

The bearded man then raised the sleeve of Willie's oversized shirt that exposed his large arm and said as he looked at Mark, "I believe you forgot something, sir."

Mark replied by asking, "What might that be?"

The bearded man looked to the people at the table and said with a grin, "A few years back there were stories of a Virginia planter, a muscle-bound slave boy and a wild mountain man named Big Sean that came through the Cumberland Gap." His grin turned into a laugh as he shook his head and said, "Well, as the stories go, this big mountain man would talk the young bucks that thought they could whip a bear into arm wrestling this slave boy. When their arms would slam against the log tables they realized they had made the wrong choice." The bearded man looked at Mark and said, "Then this Virginia planter always appeared at the right time to take control of the sometimes hostile atmosphere." The settlers and frontiersman of that time also knew just by the nod of his head this tall stern-looking man with cold black eyes could turn his friend, the wild, oversized mountain man into a machine of destruction."

Mark, by now, was across the table from the bearded man. He put his long black whip against the table next to where he would be sitting. As he sat down, he said to the bearded man who was sitting across the table from him by then, "If what you say is true then where's this wild mountain man you been talking about."

"All I now," replied the bearded man, "is there's been reports of him being in the land north of the Illinois and east of the Mississippi River."

Mark looked at Willie across the table from him with a thin smile and said, "Who knows, maybe we'll run into him sometime."

The meal went well and every one wanted to talk to Willie and Mark. Later on in the evening Mark and Dave went down by the river to the small tavern and had their drink. While they were gone one of the bigger boys in the party couldn't resist the temptation to take Willie on in an arm wrestling contest. "The evening then came to an end with Willie once again being the center of attraction."

The next morning the camp was awoken by the reddish glow to the east setting the stage for the sun to rise. The rising sun then cast it's spell upon our ancestor below marking the end of their first night in a place called Illinois. As they awoke from a contended night sleep and began dreaming of the trip ahead Mark and Willie looked at each other with a little grin as they heard from the far end of the camp the chronic sound of a rooster's crow.

Mark, Willie and the guide named John Sean left an hour before the prairie ships began to roll. The party had enough food and water to last two days and on the third day out they would be expecting game enough to feed everyone. The three men would be following an old Indian trail to a river. Willie and John Sean would then begin by displaying their hunting skills as they follow the river north in search of the selected game for their first meal in the prairie. This meal would take place a few miles from the rough terrain of the river and bottom lands allowing the prairie ships to move north on higher, leveler land. Mark was taking advantage of the opportunity to see firsthand what this new land had to offer a Virginia planter in search of free land.

At noon on the third day just as planned the three men spotted the prairie ships in the distances.

Willie looked at Mark and said, "You're right, Mark, they do look like ships on an ocean of water."

As they got closer they seen an opening in the tall grasses as the wagon train came to a stop. Everyone gathered around a smaller wagon that served some dried food, water and pastries that was prepared before their trip began. Willie and John Sean displayed the catch they had selected from the nearby woods that would be their evening meal. Again, Willie and now John Sean were the center of attraction as everyone that came by would pat them on the back and say *Good job, boys*. After the short lunch break the chuck wagon, as they called it, would leave with Willie And John Sean so they could set up for the evening meal at a selected place on their map. There they would attempt to have the meal well in process by the time the large wagons arrived.

Another reddish glow began to appear, this time to the west as the setting sun began to squeeze itself below the horizon. The wagons had gathered in a large circle around the food that had been prepared, leaving an aroma that could be smelled far from the majestic seen. The first real meal out after leaving the Ohio river was just coming to an end as the sun's last squeezes placed it out of sight below the horizon. The glowing light from the setting sun was beginning to fade, etching a permeant image in the minds of men of a time in history that would be handed down to the generation that followed.

One of the larger towns in the territory of Illinois was on the banks of the Mississippi river about thirty or forty miles west of there campsite. It was called Kaskaskia and the county seat of Randolph county at the time. It was said to have a population of about seven thousand caused by the massive influx of people going up the Mississippi and exiting into the Kaskaskia River. Some of these men were frontiersman hunting and trapping the river for trade back in town. Some of course were settlers and squatters going up the river in search of free land.

Another town on the river called Vandalia was already being considered for the Capital of the soon to be new State of Illinois. It was not for it's size it was being considered but more because of it's central location to the population at the time. Two days later the ships of the prairie came to a stop on the east side of the river across from Vandalia.

The last meal the party would share together was about to take place as Willie and John Sean began to start the fires that would cook the game they had taken from the woods. The stories of Mark, Willie and Big Sean had grown since they had left the Ohio river. Now that the party of settlers and squatters would all be going their separate ways tomorrow some were wanting to see the Virginia planter display his expertise with the long black whip. The trees beside the river was offering relief from the heat of late afternoon sun as the their last meal together came to an end. Mark felt the mood of this hardy bunch of dreamers and realized that they were searching for a moment in time that they could hang on to as they curved a path through the endless prairies and timbers of Illinois. So the next half hour was spent as the people watched Mark demonstrate how deadly accurate he was with the long black whip that was handed down to him by his father back in Virginia.

The reddish glow of the setting sun was starting to dull as Willie put his arms around a nearby tree. Mark moved closer over to the tree and the next seen that evening was of a long black whip as it snapped at Willie's back. The light left over from the setting sun was to dull to see the tip of the whip as a woman in the crowd screamed.

"Oh my God!"

Willie then turned, bowed his head and said, "Thank you, Master Mark, sir!" Willie then walked in the direction of the people with an oversize smile on his big rounded cheeks and everyone knew by then of course that Willie was okay.

Mark walked over to face the lady that had screamed and with a thin smile below his deep black eyes said, "Ma'am, I'm sorry we startled you with our tomfoolery." He then turned to the crowd that seemed to be in dismay over what they had just seen happen before their eyes and said, "You folks are writing the history for the next generation to read. So let them not forget that slavery was a real part of our lives." He then put his arm around Willie's shoulder and said, "Let them also remember that mercy given to a few gave hope to many."

The next day John Sean made his decision to go with Mark and Willie north west to a river that would become known as the Sangamon. Their map showed it flowing north then west and dumping into the Illinois river just north of an old Indian village. Some where west of the Sangamon and this Indian village now known as Beardstown lay the flat lands that Mark had heard so much about. It was refereed by some as the land of opportunity because of the timbers that stood between the lazy river and the endless miles of flat prairie land. The day then was spent gathering the necessities that they would need for their trip through the prairies and down the river to the new settlement.

The next day they traveled north west and stayed the night by a group of trees that is now called Honey Bend. Little did Mark know that his Grandson would live near this spot several years later.

As they moved north the next day they started to notice that the grasses were getting taller and the land appeared to be darker in color. The following sun set found the three men at the east edge of the prairie that Mark had been hunting for.

While Willie and John Sean were setting up camp Mark reviewed the map that he had been carrying. He noticed that there appeared to be a trail west going through the prairie to the Indian village on the Illinois river. After a closer look he also seen another trail winding its way north and intersected with the Sangamon River. This trail appeared to be going away from the prairie so Mark made the decision to follow the trail west the next day.

The next morning they got an early start and by noon they found themselfs in the hart of the prairie where the grass was higher then a man making it hard to see the horizon. As the trail appeared to narrow Mark became concerned as he had heard stories of people getting lost in the prairies. About that time he noticed it looked like a storm was brewing.

He then said as he turned around, "Willie, I think it's time for us to head back."

"What makes you think we should go back, Mark?" asked Willie.

Then they heard the roaring thunder of the storm followed by a streak of lightning. The whites of Willie's eyes seem to light up the prairie as he said, "I is getting out of here!" Willie was scared for a good reason because it was common knowledge that when lightning struck in the prairie it could burn everything in its path for miles.

IN SEARCH OF FREE LAND

When they got back to their campsite Mark realized that his father was right again when he said it would take hundreds of slaves to farm that virgin land and ship the goods down to New Orleans. After that day Mark seemed to loose his desire for the prairie.

"Little did he know that the Industrial Revolution that was soon to follow would change the looks of the prairie for ever with out the use of slaves."

The next day they headed north on the trail that would take them to the Sangamon River. Just before they got to the river the trail took them up into a wooded area. There was a garden and a small building on one side of the trail and on the other side there was a larger building where a few Indians and a few white men had gathered. Later this location would become the center of a village we now know as New Salem. It appeared as tho they were laughing and having a good time. When they dismounted from their horses Mark realized why they were having such a good time. When he saw them passing a container around, taking a drink and laughing he knew what was inside. When they got to the door the Indians had gathered around Willie as it must have been the first time they had ever seen a black man before. They were jabbering back and forth with the white men that must of known a little bit of their language. Then one of the white men came up to Willie and said "they would like to feel your arm." Willie looked at Mark and Mark nodded his head as they came up one at a time to feel his large arms. They then took another drink from the container and felt each others arms and chuck their heads no as they laughed and looked over at Willie.

Next they spotted the long black whip that was hanging on Mark's saddle horn and started to gather around the horse. Mark seen what was happening and said, "Willie, go get my whip." When the Indians saw Willie heading for the horse they all scattered. Willie took the whip over to Mark. Mark laid the tip of the whip on the ground then raised his arm up and out with such force that the sound of the snap was once again heard in the near by prairie in Illinois. While Willie was taken his oversized shirt off so the Indians could see the whip marks on his back Mark was talking to a hunter that had came out of the building when he heard the sound of the whip, thinking it was a gunshot. During their conversation the hunter informed Mark of a trail heading west through some prairie, but mostly timbers to the foot hills of the river valley. There the hunter said it will pass a small Indian tribe known as the Chick Shacks and on west to a large hill that overlooked the river valley. He then said about an hour from there you will come to the larger Indian village near the Illinois River where the hunters, trappers and settlers in the area come to trade with each other. This village would soon become known as Beardstown.

Mark was trying to make the decision whether to take the trail to the Illinois River or take the Sagamon River to the Illinois River. His original plan was to build a log raft from the abundance of timbers, sell their horses and float down the Sagamon to the Illinois to the Mississippi on their return trip home. They spent the night on the banks of the Sagamon and the next morning John Sean made his decision to stay in the area. He agreed with Mark that the Indian village on the Illinois would probably be a good place to market his furs.

They all spent the next few days hunting, fishing and feasting. The hunter named Bill that Mark was talking to up on the hill could communicate with the Indians enough to have some of them to agree to take Mark And Willie with them to meet their Chief.

Mark, Willie and John Sean said their goodbyes. John Sean was waving laughing and shaking his head as he seen Mark and Willie following the small group of Indians over the hill and out of sight. After traveling through a small prairie the trail took them through some hilly land and them dropped down into the foothills of the Sagamon River bottom next to some Indians Mounds where their village was nested. Of course the little Indian village came a live when they seen maybe for their first time a black man dismount from his horse. The young bucks that brought them were talking to the Chief as he raised his arm and motion for them to come forward. He raised his hand and made a motion to welcome them. He then made another motion for Willie to remove his shirt. Willie looked a Mark and Mark nodded his head yes. The Chief motioned for Willie to turn around as he gazed at his shinny black back that was covered with scares. His still gray eyes came in contact with Mark's snappy black eyes and nether man spoke for a few seconds.

He then raised his arm and pointed to the saddle on the horse where the black whip was hanging as he looked back at Mark and said with a motion of his arm, "Bring."

Mark looked at Willie and pointed to the horse and said, "Bring me the whip, Willie."

The Chief knew by now that Mark must be a Chief in the white mans land and commanded dominate rule. Willie had brought the whip over to Mark and placed it on the ground in front of him. He then stepped a few steps in front of Mark and stopped. Mark picked the whip up and said, "One more step, Willie," and then the sound from the snap of the whip echoed through the hill of the little Indian village. Willie then turned and walked back to stand beside Mark. Mark then put his arm around Willie's shoulder and then put his hands together above his head and said, "Now free," as he open up his hands as to release a bird into the wide open spaces. He then open and closed his hands as if the bird was flying away. The Chief seem to know by now that the black man was not only free but big medicine in the white mans world.

They were asked to set at the fire and eat. While Mark sent the next few hours try to communicate with the Chief Willie was getting all the attention as the small younger bucks were by then feeling the black mans mighty arms. Willie would then lay on the ground on his belly and let the little ones push his large arm into the ground. Then every one in the camp would laugh, but none of the older braves would challenge the large black arm of Willie. After rubbing of their belles and making sounds of contentment they mounted their horses and made gesture of goodbye with their arms as they rode off west to look for the large hill over looking the river bottom land.

The sun was getting close to the horizon in the west as they caught the first view of the large hill that seem to be standing guard over the valley below. The direction of travel, the height of the sun and the colors of the hillside gave off a majestic view that seem to attract Mark to move closer in it's direction. He then knew he couldn't go any further until he stood on top and claimed the land below. After looking out over the valley below Mark and Willie turned and looked at each other.

Mark then said, "Willie, man will come and claim this land soon, but for now all that lay from here to the river and as far as we can see is ours and it's free."

The hill they were standing on is now a cemetery that over looks the town of Chandlerville.

Mark looked at Willie again and said, "You know, Willie, I believe I have found my dream." He was silent for a moment as he gazed out over the valley below and said, "But for some strange reason I don't really have a desire to claim it and put it in my pocket." With a gleam in his black eyes, he said, "Instead, let us pass this memory on to the next generation so they to can enjoy such a view."

Willie looked out over the valley below and said, "Mark, this is what real freedom is all about, isn't it."

Mark's thin smile turned into a big grin as he said, "And we both found it together, didn't we?"

They spent the night on the hilltop then the next morning as the sun peaked its eye over the ridge Mark and Willie gave up their claim on the land below as they rode off to the west following the foothills to Mound Village near the Illinois River.

A short while later in a place that the French had named Beautiful Mound Village, two men on horseback rode in. One was a white man on a black horse and one was black man on a white horse.

The Indians that were mingling with the white traders looked up in dismay as they cast their eyes upon the first black man that they had ever seen. Both men dismounted from their horses and Mark began talking to the white men Willie of course was being investigated by the Indians. Mark spent the rest of the day with traders and hunters as they loaded their goods onto a large boat that would be leaving out the next day for the long trip down the Illinois to the Mississippi and then to New Orleans.

Mark and Willie sold their horses for good profit and Willie signed on to help the captain man the boat down the river. Mark paid for a fare that would take him to a village just north of where the Ohio dumped into the Mississippi. There the two me would buy two horse and cross the tip of southern Illinois to the Ohio River.

After they made all their arrangements and new about what time they would arrive home back in Kentucky, Mark, for the first time in serval days, realized how much he missed his Sarah.

They were all standing by a fire near a tent shack that was set up for trading when one of the old story tellers stared telling stories about the old days. Soon he was heard telling a story about a giant of a man named Big Sean. His hair he said hung below his shoulders and when he talked the roar of his voice came out sounding like a mountain lion in heat.

The old timer smiled a little as he knew by now he had captured every ones attention. He then said that mountain man had a large nose and could smell the sent of animal a day after he passed through the woods. It has been said by those who knew him that even the bears would hide behind trees down wind from him to keep him from picking up their sent.

By now a small boy that was standing by the fire, was over, hanging onto his dad's pant leg.

Mark and Willie both looked at each other at the same time as Mark said, "Say, old timer, you don't happen to know where that mountain man came from, do you?"

"Not for sure," replied the old man, "but there's been stories about him coming out of them there blue ridge mountains down in Virginia."

"Have there been any reports of that mountain man in this part of the country," asked Mark as he stepped out where the old timer could see him?

"Why, yes," replied the old-timer as he rubbed his old gray beard with a weather beaten hand. "It seems," he said, "that he passed through here about two years ago." By this time, the old man spotted Willie standing behind Mark. A little grin peaked through his fluffy gray beard as he said, "While that big mountain man was here he whipped three men with one hand tied behind his back." He hesitated a moment then shook his old gray head and said, "When they untied that big old mountain man's hands, he let out a roar that was heard way down there at that Mississippi River. Then he claimed that the only man that could whip him was a big slave boy that grew up east of them there Blue Ridge Mountains."

Of course, by then the people that were gathered around the fire were looking at Willie and began to notice how large his arms were. They also new that Willie was traveling with Mark and had seen the long black whip hanging on the saddle on Mark's horse. Within the hour one of the hunters from Kentucky was telling stories of a Virginia planter and his musclebound slave that had come through the Cumberland Gap with a roaring mountain man they called Big Sean.

Before the night came to an end the sound of the long black whip was once again heard in the remote area of the Illinois frontier. After each sound form the snap of the long black whip came the hand clads showing approval for the entertainment for the evening. By then, of course, the local Indian bucks were getting to much of the white man's joy juice and thought they could put the big black arm of Willie's into the dirt on the ground. The sporting event that evening took place as they would lie belly down on the ground with elbows together waiting for the sound from the snap of the long black whip. As the disappointed Indians fell off to sleep, the only sound heard on the banks of the river bottom was that of a lonely wolf in the nearby timbers.

Once again, the rising sun would cast its spell upon two men, one white and one black, as they stood on the deck of a large wooden boat and watched as their dream slowly disappeared behind them. Mark new by now that the beauty of the lonely prairie would not gave in easily to man and his plow. Little did Mark know at that time that Willie would be the one who would set his plow deep in the Illinois prairie as one of the first settlers to attempt the challenge.

The disappointment of the prairie had caused Mark to think back to a time that now seemed so long ago. There in his mind appeared Sarah as she ran to the barn, her hair flowing in the breeze and her dress wrapping around the curves of her well developed body. Without thinking, Mark said out loud, "Willie, it's time to go home."

Willie replied with what Mark thought was a strange answer at the time as he said, "I feel like I'm leaving home, Master Mark."

IN SEARCH OF FREE LAND

A few days later after serval stops alone the way they floated through an area where the two rivers came together to form one called the mighty Mississippi. Shortly the large wooden boat was skillfully maneuvered over to the western bank of the mighty river. There they would tie off and spend the night in a small boom town called St. Louis.

Some of the furs that was loaded up on the Illinois river were being unloaded at a few of the local merchants. Mark had nothing to do and found himself helping Willie deliver the furs. Mark and Willie were walking back to the boat with two other mem as they came upon a tavern that appeared to be very active inside. They all stopped as if they were deciding if they wanted to go in or go on to the next one. Suddenly the door popped opened and out came a man landing at the feet of Mark. Willie was by his side as they both looked up and saw the huge body of a wild looking mountain man.

Next they heard the loud roar of his voice say, "And you best be out of town when I come out." He then looked down and saw a pare of white eyes looking at him from the dark street. When he saw the large arms hanging from his big shoulders he realized it was Willie. Then he said, "Hey, boy, are trying to spook me?" About that time he jumped out of the door way and grabbed Willie so quick he didn't know what had happened. The next thing Willie knew he was being squeezed so had that he couldn't hardly get his breath. When Willie's feet touched the ground he turned to Mark shook his hand and said, "Damn, it's good to see the both of you."

Shortly all of men were standing near the bar in a fairly large tavern for town of its size. When Mark looked around the room he noticed that there were other men dressed similar to Big Sean. After a short time he realized they were mountain men, too. Some would soon be going up the Missouri following the trail that Lewis & Clark had made famous a few years earlier. Some were coming from the famous trail with the abundances of fine furs to sell to the merchants in the fast growing boomtown that would soon be known as the gateway to the west.

As the evening pass by Mark found out that Big Sean was about to head north up the Missouri on his second trip to a land where the mountains seemed to reach the heavens. Only a few men dared to enter the lands where the giant mountains seem to never end. The ones that did were called mountain men.

Mark watched as the large roaring mountain man put his arms around Willie showing him off to the crowd that had gather. Mark realized by now that the bond between the two men was to great for them to inter into an arm wrestling contest that may jeopardize their friendship.

He may have been right because a short time later a small grin appeared from within the big bushy beard of Big Sean as he asked Willie if he remembered what he said when he left Kentucky.

Willie answered with a bigger grin by saying, "It seems to me, sir, you said when I grew up maybe I could take on a real mountain, man."

Big Sean let out a roar and said, "There it is, boys, now who's going to take on the little black boy here."

They both were off the hook and didn't have to face each other.

A big bushy bearded men began to walk around Willie and noticed that he was no little boy.

Big Sean said take off your shirt boy so they can take a good look. After they observed his large shinny black arm and seen the whip marks on his powerful looking back the line of men around him became smaller.

One man near the size of Big Sean didn't set down, but instead roared out in a voice that seemed to shake the room and said, "Let's get this show on the road."

Big Sean said in a loud voice, "Not until all the bets are down."

The big man was setting across the table from Willie when he laughed and said to Big Sean, "Can I keep him when I beat him?"

"Not unless you think you can whip me!" roared Big Sean.

The big man let out with a chuckle from his loud voice as he looked at Willie and said, "I don't need a slave, anyway."

Willie looked deep in the big mans eyes and said in a determine voice. "I am a free man, sir!"

Go was still ringing in the ears of the bystanders from the loud voice of Big Sean as the two men from two different worlds arms began to move first one way and then the other. The huge arm of the wild looking mountain man that was known only as wild Bill said, "Okay, free man, hang on. It's time for your whipping."

Wild Bill's body appeared much larger than Willie's, but would not help him at the table where only the arm could be used. The years of living in the land of giant mountains where the mighty grisly and the savage Indians roamed of course forced his instinct for survival to be highly active. This allowed him to get the snap on Willie's wrist and began to move the muscular black arm ever so slowly in the direction of the tabletop.

The one time slave boy grew up under the long days of hard work and as a free man years of log splitting in Kentucky. The well condition muscular arm of Willie was just to much for wild Bill to hold. Then slowly their arms came up pass center. Wild Bills arm held for a moment and then gave in to the powerful arm of Willie. When the mighty arm of the wild mountain man slammed into the table the bystanders new that Willie was not just a slave boy but a legend in the avenue of the giants.

Wild Bill started to push his big body up from the chair he was setting on when a large hand on his shoulder pushed down. He then turned his head and looked up into a large hand that had been rolled into a fist, cocked and ready to shoot downward on command.

Wild Bill had once tried Big Sean on for size and soon found out the hard way that it was a mistake. He never believed in making the same mistake twice, so he said, "I was just going to shake the hand of that free man over there."

The next day their paths would part never to cross again as the boat carrying Big Sean and wild Bill began its slow journey up the Missouri and then to a land where only a few men dare to go. Mark and Willie were standing on the back of a boat looking up river as they traveled rapidly down river on the mighty Mississippi that would take them closer to their home in Kentucky.

In less than a week the two men one black and one white but both with an overdose of freedom flowing through their blood were setting on their horses on a ridge in Kentucky. They were looking down into a valley that a few years back that they claimed for their home, but now it looked so civilized.

At the end of the day Mark's wondering feet came to rest as he removed his boots and placed them at the end of their bed. Sarah was already lying in bed in a nightgown that she had ordered just for this occasion. It was partly open in the front leaving little for the imagination, but enough to stir the inter workings of a lonely man with wondering feet but still deeply in love. After tearing all the buttons from his shirt and pants, he heard a swirling breeze sweep though the valley below as Sarah gently laid the blankets aside so Mark could inter. The violence of the storm finally came to an end as the sound of contentment once again was heard riding the breeze of the midnight air. After the storm they pulled the covers up to their necks as they looked deep into each others eyes. A smile began to appear on their faces as their lips gently touched causing the bodies to mingle below the sheets.

Mark's thin smile displayed a touch of devilment as he winked and said, "Round two."

Sarah smiled back as she ran her fingers through his black wavy hair and said, "I double dare you."

Mark willingly excepted the dare and shortly the long night came to an end as the rising sun peaked through the window.

Chapter Twenty
Willie Leaves for Illinois

The following years passed by fast and Mark keep his wondering feet planted in the Kentucky soil. Willie had gather a good size nest egg and was spending a lot of time working for a family from South Carolina.

Then one day Willie came to visit Mark and said his goodbyes as he would be going north into Illinois with the family from South Carolina, the Cox family and a few other families from that area. They both reached out to shake hands as Mark said, "Willie, a handshake won't do it," and then they embraced each other with a hug.

Mark's son, young William, was about 7 years old by then and said, "We're going to miss you, Willie."

Willie was on his horse ready to turn to leave when Sarah came out. She was standing by Mark holding his hand as she waved and said, "You'll always be in our hearts, Willie."

With a tear in his eye, Willie turned and rode off out of sight.

Mark had talked to Eli Cox a few days before that and was told that they may be settling near the area that him and Willie had explored on their trip to Illinois. Mark realized after having his last visit with Elie that it would take men like him and Willie with smaller dreams but endless determination to cultivate the black dirt that lay below the tall grasses of the Illinois prairie.

Chapter Twenty-One
Mark and Sarah's Leave for Illinois

Over the next few years young William now known as Bill began changing into a young man. Little did he know at the time while hunting in the timbers and working in the fields of Kentucky that he would inherit the wondering feet of his father.

Mark and Sarah had done well in Kentucky and didn't really have to work to make a living anymore so they made their decision to rent their land out to a relative from Virginia and go to Illinois.

The year was 1831, young Bill was 17 and would stay at home to help take care of the family farm while his mother and father took a well deserved trip by themselfs.

Mark and Sarah found themselfs going down the Ohio in a steamer in search of free land. This time with his beloved Sarah by his side. Their trip had began in Golconda where Mark and Willie began their exploratory journey serval years earlier. This time instead of following the trail through the endless prairie they would follow the river on a steamer down the Ohio and up the Mississippi.

The smoke was rising from the stack of the steamer and drifting of into the country side as they began their long journey up the Mississippi. The trip took them by the mouth of the famous Kaskaskia River where thousands of hunters, settlers and squatters moved up and planted the seeds of growth in the new state. The sun was drafting downward in the west as the boat came to rest for the evening in a place called St. Louis.

Of course Mark and Sarah both were over excited hoping for the possibility of seeing Big Sean. By now the boom town was becoming the crossroads for the daring men and women of the new frontier west of the Mississippi. The town had grown since Mark and Willie were there and now offered a selection of dining and entertainment. After their disappointment of not seeing Big Sean they took their dinner at the best restaurant in town.

The next morning the swirling smoke from the steamers chimney produced an artistic view of the area as it was stirred to the right off the Mississippi onto the Illinois river.

The next stop was the Indian village called Mound City by the French but now known as Beardstown. Mark and Sarah settled near the hill that him and Willie had claimed for theirs for the night on their exploratory trip a few years earlier.

Sarah fell in love with the view and Mark seemed contended for the first time since he left Virginia. As they stood on top of the hill overlooking the valley below Sarah put her arms around Mark's waist and leaned back gently. When her deep blue eyes looked into his black snappy eyes, his thin smile appeared as he said, "Would you care to make this our new Home." Both their memories were spinning back to their first night after they were married in their log cabin called paradise. Sarah swung her head back and to the side to allow her hair to blow in the breeze as she looked up at Mark and said, "I double dare you!"

Again Mark excepted the dare as darkness fell upon the hill. The rumbling tumbling noise of the restless night finally came to an end as a lonely wolf gave one last how for the evening. Mark and Sarah fell into a contended sleep on the hilltop locked in each others arms. When they awoke, Mark's desire to go in search of free land was there no more.

They built a small log cabin near their majestic hill with the help of John Sean and a few of his friends. John Sean was the man that helped

Willie hunt for game to feed the party of settlers and squatters when they came up through Illinois in prairie ships a few years earlier. He now lived about halfway between their majestic hill and a new town that was called New Salem. There were rumors that Willie settled south west of New Salem in the hart of the prairie and was married to a white woman.

Mark's talent for buying and selling and being at the right place at the right time allow them to live very well in the remote area of the frontier. The next year or two they spent traveling to from the remote towns that were springing up in the wooded areas near the endless miles of prairie. Serval trips took them through the hart of the prairie to visit Willie where they would reminisce about the good old days. At the end of all their visits Willie would look up at the sky and say, "I wonder where that big man ended up at." Their last visit to the prairie to see Willie and his family ended with Willie rasing his large black arm to wave goodbye to his one time master and now his best friend. When the horse and buggy began to inter into the path of the tall grass of the prairie Mark pulled back on the reins as both he and Sarah looked back into the opening that Willie called a farm. There before their eyes they saw Willie with the reins around his big wide shoulders as the horse pulled the plow that was turning up the bright black dirt of the untamed prairie. His kids were following behind walking in the furrow of the fresh plowed ground. Mark turned to Sarah and said honey wouldn't his mom and dad be proud of him now? You know he said he is cutting a path for the white man to follow.

Sarah looked into the deep black eyes of her man and said, "And just who do you think was responsible for that?"

As their buggy entered the path of the tall grass they both turned to look back over their shoulders and seen that the prairie appeared to have swallowed. Willie and his farm.

One of their trips to New Salem they meet a young man named Abe Lincoln. Other trips took them up the Illinois to the town of Peoria. The love affair with the frontier was about to come to an end as their desire to go back to their Kentucky home began to set in. They spent the last night on their majestic hill locked in each others arms overlooking the valley below as they heard the farewell sound of a lonely wolf. They awoke the next morning and decided this would be their temporary home when Mark had a desire to wonder from the routine of the farm life in Kentucky.

Chapter Twenty-Two
Young William Moves to Illinois

A few years later back in Kentucky young Bill got the itch to see what lay beyond the sunset. Then one morning Mark and Sarah and the rest of the family found then self's waving goodbye as Bill left his Kentucky home going in the direction of the state of Illinois. He never got far enough north to see Willie but as he wondered he did find the love of his life.

Like a long distance relay time had past the first generation of Cooper's from the state of Virginia to the new state of Illinois. It was near the town of Carrollton when the baton, a leather case holding the long black whip, was handed over to the next generation of Cooper's. It happened on April 22, 1846, shortly after the young William son of Mark looked deep into the eyes of a young lady named Elizabeth Duncan and said, "I do." The preacher then pronounced them man and wife. Then later on in the evening when the gifts were handed out the last gift they open was the black leather case holding the long black whip. When Mr. And Mrs. William Cooper opened the case they pulled out a hand painted picture of his father and Willie.

It seems that while watching one of the demonstration that Mark and Willie put on when they made their exploratory trip up through Illinois, there was a country artist who recorded the event. In the picture Willie had his arms around a tree, his shirt was off to expose his muscular body and his head was back to give the appearance of him begging for mercy. A tall man in a white shirt with black wavy hair and deep black eyes was portrayed holding a long black whip. The tip of the whip that touched the back of black shiny body appeared to be drawing blood.

Young William then pulled the long black whip from the case as he looked over at a man with black wavy hair that by now had streaks of gray in it and said, "Thanks, Dad."

His father Mark put his arms around his big shoulders and said, "Take care of the whip and hand it down to your son." Then he looked at his son through his black snappy eyes and said, "That way his generation shall remember it as a tool of injustice and that slavery did indeed exist." He then said, "Your mother and I will be leaving soon to go back to Kentucky." With a thin smile that appeared to be closer to a large grin he said, "By the way, Willie is still married to a white woman and lives in the prairie near Springfield."

The second lap of the search for fee land would soon begin as the land west of the Mississippi became more and more populated. Mountain men like Big Sean and his friends were no more just memories of the past, but a recorded legend in the history of a mighty nation. The prairie was still dominated by the forces of nature as the oceans of grass swayed by the gentle winds passing through the lonely land. Only a few like Willie had dared to try to inter the ocean of grass, plant their roots deep in the ground and call it home. The industrial revolution was about to change the ocean of grass into the bread basket of the world. The giant fields of corn, wheat and oats would some day replace the oceans of grass and the lonely prairie would be no more.

Bill and Elizabeth began their life on land near the spot where his father and Willie had camped for the night serval years earlier now called Honey Bend. Bill was now 32 years old and was said by those that new, that he looked a lot like his grandfather Will. He was a large man with a jolly personality and it has been said that he would rather fight then eat. But after his marriage to Liz as he called her, his apatite got larger and his desire to fight got smaller.

Liz was a small lady with dark hair, bright sparkling eyes and a quick temper. She believed furiously in the lord and would not allow his name to be used in fain.

Bill's barroom brawling and Liz's religion of course didn't set the stage for the perfect marriage. But between the yelling and the screaming their were the moments of wild desires and moments of contentment and peace. Their love affair would last until her death in1864.

Bill tried to learn the expertise of handling the long black whip like his father before him but never mastered it to that extent. It was just as well he didn't as Illinois was by then a free state. During his tenure of the whip, it's home would be resting in a slot close to his hand on the front of their buggy. On their weekly trips to town on Sat, the big sandy haired Bill would snap the whip at the rear of the horses to make them strut. Liz could be seen shaking her finger in his face, saying, "That will be enough of that, Bill Cooper."

Eight years passed by as Bill etched out a living between some farming some hunting and trapping. But his fun loving ways and a few more mouths to feed didn't allow for a lot of saving. So he made the decision to go north to Cass county near the area where his father and Willie had ended their exploratory trip serval years before.

After a few fights with Liz and his reluctance to go to church the Preacher was heard saying, "Thanks for coming to our service, Bill, and the best luck to you and your family on your trip north."

The congregation were waving their hands goodbye as the wagon wheels began to move leaving their marks in the black dirt of the prairie

The Cooper family had once again began their trip in search of free land. Within a few weeks Bill Cooper Ent. Into the records a grant for thirty-eight acres near the settlement of Newmansville.

The settlers by then were beginning to build their homes further away from the safety of the Timbers and closer to the land they were trying to farm. Due to the industrial revolution larger strips of the prairie grass was being turn over each year giving small section of the prairie a civilized complection.

After their home was built from the trees of the near by timbers they began taking short trips. Brawling Bill as he was called would ride through the tall prairie grass on his way to a new settlement in search of a local tavern to quench his addictive thirst, but on Sabbath he would be seen in his Sunday best with Liz by his side and the long black whip hanging in it's resting place on the front of the buggy.

One Sunday as they entered the church next to a school house on the edge of the prairie. The preacher said welcome to Bill, Liz and their two boys. He put his hand on Bill's shoulder and said, "Will you stay around after the services, as I have something I want to say to you?"

The services seemed to be centered around the evil of man. One of the prayers made note of the belief that God created all men equal. When all the people had left the church yard the preacher came over to Bill and Liz and said, "I have some sad news for you."

"What could that be?" asked Bill as he looked at Liz.

The preacher then said, "Bill, do you remember when you and Liz first came to our church?"

"Yes," replied Bill.

You said then that you had been looking for a black man named Willie that was married to a white woman. You said that your father had told you that he had settled some where near Springfield in the early eighteen hundreds and was attempting to farm the prairies. Then after months of searching you indicated to me that you had no luck in finding him. While we were talking that first time you also told me about this Willie being your fathers slave and had earned his freedom in the frontiers of Kentucky splitting logs and arm wrestling all that dare to take him on. He then held his head down for a moment as if to find the right words to say. Then he looked up and said, "The stories of your father, Willie and the long black whip seem to make Willie more family than slave." Then as he looked into their eyes he said, "Your Willie has been found. He has entered the halls of history for ever and his body has been placed in the roots of the prairie. It was reported that some of his last words that came from his lips were Master Will, brother Mark and Big Sean. Then when his eyes close with his last breath of life he uttered the words I's a free man."

Bill thought for a moment and said with a tear in his eyes, "My dad once told me when I was a little boy back in Kentucky that the roots of the Illinois prairie would someday feed the world. Then, shortly after that, Willie left with some other settlers to go north to the Illinois prairie. I can still remember," he said as he looked at the preacher, "my dad with a big smile on his face, saying to my mom, that Willie Boy's about to write his name in the history books using a one-horse walking plow instead of a pen."

Bill and Liz done well the next few years between his hunting, trapping and farming the small farm on the edge of the prairie. During the long winter nights sometimes the passion in the bedroom of the frontier house at the edge of the prairie got out of control and soon another addition would be added to the Cooper Family. Bills trips to the taverns in the area became less but the name Brawling Bill could still be heard as they talked about his fights. The tale that was told most was of the three men that made the mistake of saying something derogatory about a free black man named Willie. From that day forward, the men that new him kept their feelings about Willie to themselves in his presence.

In 1859 Bill sold his land and settled nearby where he continued to hunt, fish, farm, and squeeze in a fight or two on his benders to the local taverns.

The long nights of the cold winters and the need for more help in the fields in the summer months caused the family to grow to eight children. They consisted of six boys and two girls by the time their mother past away in 1864.

One of their sons a fifteen year old named Alexander would live be the only son to be buried in the roots of the Illinois prairies. The other brothers had inherited the wondering feed of their grandfather Mark but were still to young to spread their wings.

A year later Bill married another Elizabeth this time her last name was Blunt. She brought into the Cooper family one son, making them a total of nine. Within the next ten years the family grew to thirteen.

Chapter Twenty-Three
Death to the Legend of the Long Black Whip

During that time in history young Alexander known by then as Alex, married Ann Barrett in Oct. 1869. Once again the baton, the black box that held the long black whip, the hand painted picture of his grandfather Mark and his one time slave named Willie, was handed over to the next generation. Alex hung the whip in a slot on the buggy like his father before him. It would rest there for show only but those that new him well new he could and would use it if the occasion called for it.

The occasion did come to past a few years later. "As the story goes Alex was away on a bridge job, when a male teacher that lived in the nearby town and teaching in a small country school whip one of his daughters to the extent that it left marks on her back. When the teacher returned to town that evening the word got out about what had happened at the school, the teacher was told by one of the towns people, that he best catch the first train out of town before Big Al comes to town with that whip of his.

The next scene of the story reports a school teacher on a train going out of town as Big Al Cooper came rushing through town in his fancy buggy and a long black whip in his hand. When he got to the train station he pulled the sweaty lathered up team of horses to a stop. He then stood up with the whip in his hand and saw the black smoke from the train rising above the tree tops on it's way out of town.

It has been said that when he stop and thought about what he almost done he realized that the legend of the long black whip must die. So the next day he took it to a near by gravesite and buried at the foot of a grave that held the remains of Willie's body. There in the roots of the Illinois prairies they both would lie in peace never to be seen again."

Shortly after that his grandfather Mark and grandmother Sarah died and were buried close to their beloved hill over looking the well remember river and the valley below.

There was rumors during that period of time that Big Sean was killed by a large bear some where in the high mountains west of the Mississippi.

Over time the grasses from the endless prairies and the giant rocks of the mighty mountains would consume the remains of a generation leaving only bits and pieces of fact, but a book full of imagination.

Chapter Twenty-Four
West to the Oklahoma Territory

The memories of the early eighteen hundreds was coming to and end but the burning desire to see what lay beyond the sunset was glowing bright as the new generation began moving west in search of free land.

Roaring Bill's son Sam began to fill his father's shoes as he had acquired an apatite for women, booze and a good fight. Alex son of Bill stayed put in a place called home while his father and most of his brothers follow the stars across the mighty Mississippi into the new states Missouri, Kansas and Nebr. Their they would make the names Wellington, Kansas, Chanute, Kansas and Blue Springs, Nebraska, household names in the Cooper Family as they went in search of free land.

A few years later back in Illinois in 1880, roaring Bill Cooper at the age of 66 was running a hotel in Virginia, Illinois, telling the stories of his sons out in the wild west.

Alex and Ann were an unusual couple as he was a very large man and she was a very small lady. He wore a mustache and looked at you through squinty dark eyes that were reset above high cheekbones and a full face. He looked to be heavy but not fat.

Ann on the other hand was very small and her eyes could be used as a knife if she was unhappy but sparkle like the due of an early morning frost if she approved. Lucky for Alex she approved of his personality. As time passed by their family would grow to the count of five. The boys were Oscar, Nate and Arley. The girls were Loulla and Mary. Alex and his family farmed eighty acres and it is also said that he built most of the first old Iron beam bridges in cast county.

One of the tells that were floating around at the time was that he could single handedly lift an eight hundred pound pile driver. Whether this is true or not of course will never be known but one thing we do know that he was not a hostile man and did not spend all his time in a barroom. But as late as the 1940s, their were memories from old folks in the town of Chandlerville, telling about the time a huge man named Alex Cooper came into the local tavern and sat down. When the bartender brought the drink and sat it in fount of Alex, he said, "Can I ask you a question, sir?"

"Go ahead," replied the big man. "I'll answer it if I can."

The bartender said, "Well, sir, there has been reports around telling how strong you are and by the looks of your hands they may be right." Then he looked at the big man and said with a smile on his face, "If you were to hit someone with that hunk of meat called a fist and he didn't go down just what would you do?"

It is said that Big Al as some called him squeezed out a thin smile as he looked at the bartender with a glare in his squinty eyes and said, "Then I would have to get up and go look behind him to see what could be holding him up." His thin smile turned into a large chuckle as he said, "Now if I hit someone with this," as he held up his large arm, "and they don't go down and there's nothing holding them up. I would say, I'd be a fool to stick around, wouldn't you?" Everyone in the tavern were laughing as the big man got up, put some money on the bar and said, "The drinks are on me and have a good day, gentlemen."

From that day forth, the name Alexander Cooper was highly respected not only by the business community, but by the rough necks of the hills and hollows in a remote area of the new frontier.

The stories of the roaring west, free land in Oklahoma and maybe the need for money from the families out west caused Alexander to pull up stakes in Illinois and move the family to a place near Wellington Kansas. Roaring Bill was now nearing seventy five years old and left his home in Virginia, Illinois, to go with his son, Alex, only to watch his sons claim their free land. There they made the decision that some of the brothers would go with Sam and attempt to claim and hold one hundred and sixty acres near a small trading center now known as Enid in the county of Garfield. They may have been Sooner's either legal or illegal as it is common knowledge that there wasn't enough law enforcement to police the massive amount of land that was to be claimed.

"Stories did filter down to the next generation as later on, Arley, son of Alex, would tell about the gun fights in the Oklahoma territory as his family went in search of free land."

It was agreed before the race began in eighteen eighty nine that brother George would try to plant his stake in the ground in an area now known as Woodward County. It would be to the west of where Sam and the other brothers would be. Alex and his father Bill would set their stake far to the west in what is now called Cimarron County. "The search for free land that began almost one hundred years ago in the imagination of two young boys one white and one black was a about to come to an end. The search began east of the blue ridge mountains when a black slave boy named Willie looked at a local paper and said with a big smile on his face, Mark it says here there's free land west of the blue ridge!"

The powerful arm of Alexander Cooper drove his stake deep into the desalinate land of the Oklahoma territory just as two men on horses rode up and stopped. One man began to swing his leg over the saddle as the huge hands of Alex grabbed his body and flung him through the air like a basketball player throwing a basketball to his team mate. The other man's hand started for his gun when the voice of Alex's father, Roaring Bill was heard. He was by now holding a long barrel gun that was pointed at them.

He said in a voice that could be heard by the other man who was by now starting to get up, "My very large son here has a very short temper and it would be best for you to take your friend and leave while you can!"

According to legend's Alex may have sold water rights to some of the cattle drives through the panhandle of the Oklahoma Territory going to the market centers in Kansas. Whatever may have happened then it is believed that he soon grew tired of the fight for survival and sold his land and came back to Illinois to a place he called God's Country. Later on oil was found in the area and it is believed his granddaughter received oil rites not knowing it may have been her grandfather's land originally.

Sam and his brother Henry continued to live near Wellington Kansas. It was during this period of time that the son of Alex named Arley Arthur the youngest of the prospers family and not needed on the farm back in Illinois as much as the other two brothers, was given the opportunity to go visit his uncle Sam in Wellington Kansas once a year. There he got to know his cousin Fred, son of Sam very well when he was growing up as a boy. "Later on in life, Fred would become very instrumental in the world of aviation and became wealthy."

Chapter Twenty-Five
The Whispering Sounds from the Past

The train had become the mode of transportation out to the new frontier of the old west. When young Arley would return, he would tell all that would listen the stories of cowboys, gun fights and the giant rabbits that roamed the range. He became well known as a story teller and of course some of the stories were true. Some tho were articulated extremely well and were designed to tingle the imagination. Those that were true some how made it through alone with the mythical legends into the next generation.

Arley Arthur was unique to say the lest. He was a poor farmer that may have spent too much time looking up at the bottom side of an empty bottle. When he wasn't casting spells from the contains of the bottle he could be found in the fields of a well tended farm, trading horses or telling stories. He only went in search of a full bottle after wheat harvest and corn harvest.

During the dry times on Sat. night in the 1940s at the back of a store in the little town of Candlerville, the farmers would gather and leave from their to go home to their farms. There the old man would some times tell stories while the children watch in awe. The stories were some times funny but mostly scary as you could tell when kids held on tight to their mom and dads as they walked out into the dark of night to go to their farms.

Some of the stories that may have been true, was about his uncles holding their claim by force near the present day Enid Oklahoma. Another one may have been my grandfather Alex as he drove his stake deep into the ground in the panhandle of Oklahoma and challenged any man that would dare to try and jump his claim. My father Arley then told how the two men rushed to leave that had tried to jump his claim. He would always smile as he said then your great grandfather roaring Bill Cooper walked over to read the sign that was attached to the stake in the ground. As he read those words on the sign the roar in his voice was so loud that the frequency of the words were carried down through the generation. Then with the smile gone from his face he would say in a low tone of voice, "Now if you look up at the stars on your way home, close your eyes and listen. Some of you may even feel a vibration on your eardrums and hear a faint sound as roaring Bill whispers to you the words on the sign."

Of course, we didn't hear roaring Bill's voice that night, but I'm sure that we all saw the same stars that my Great Grandfather Bill and my Grandfather Alex seen over fifty years ago.

It was about sixty years later at the turn of the century in the year two thousand and three while visiting my son and family in England I was telling my grand daughter Sydney and grandson Trace a story about their ancestors and their burning desire to claim free land. They both said about the same time, why don't you write a story about their adventures. Then shortly Trace brought me a pencil and said, "Here's a pencil to write your story with Grandpa." They both then went into the next room to play.

I then put the pencil over my ear and thought to myself, you know it would be nice to write a story for them about their ancestors that they could read when they got older. A thin smile appeared on my lips as I closed my eyes and reached up to take the pencil from my ear to begin to write. As I touched the pencil I felt a slight vibration on my ear drum. Then from out of the past with my eyes still closed appeared a stake in the ground with a sign attached. When I attempted to read the sign I felt a tiny distance roaring noise in my ear, like a small gust of wind passing gently through a grove of trees on a calm night. Then I heard ever so faint the whispering words from a forgotten time. " The Cooper's last search for free land."